D1547273

ONCE IN A LIFETIME

SAPPHIRE BAY, BOOK 2

LEEANNA MORGAN

WELCOME TO SAPPHIRE BAY!

Nestled against the shore of Flathead Lake, Montana, you'll find the imaginary town of Sapphire Bay. Here you'll discover a community with big hearts, warm smiles, and lots of wonderful stories to be told. Romance, adventure, and intrigue are all waiting for you! Let's explore Sapphire Bay together in *Once In a Lifetime*, the second book in the Sapphire Bay series.

ABOUT THIS BOOK

Samantha Jones works at Fletcher Security. She develops state-of-the-art surveillance drones, hacks computer networks, and makes life difficult for anyone on the wrong side of the law.

When she's asked to help Caleb Andrews complete a top-secret project, her IT skills aren't the only thing that will be tested to the limit. Someone wants the program Caleb has created—and they'll stop at nothing to get it.

Once In A Lifetime is the second book in the Sapphire Bay series and can easily be read as a standalone. Each of Leeanna's series are linked so you can find out what happens to your favorite characters in other books. For news of my latest releases, please visit leeannamorgan.com and sign up for my newsletter. Happy reading!

Other Novels by Leeanna Morgan:

Montana Brides:
Book 1: Forever Dreams (Gracie and Trent)
Book 2: Forever in Love (Amy and Nathan)
Book 3: Forever After (Nicky and Sam)
Book 4: Forever Wishes (Erin and Jake)
Book 5: Forever Santa (A Montana Brides Christmas Novella)
Book 6: Forever Cowboy (Emily and Alex)
Book 7: Forever Together (Kate and Dan)
Book 8: Forever and a Day (Sarah and Jordan)

Montana Brides Boxed Set: Books 1-3
Montana Brides Boxed Set: Books 4-6

The Bridesmaids Club:
Book 1: All of Me (Tess and Logan)
Book 2: Loving You (Annie and Dylan)
Book 3: Head Over Heels (Sally and Todd)
Book 4: Sweet on You (Molly and Jacob)
The Bridesmaids Club: Books 1-3

Emerald Lake Billionaires:
Book 1: Sealed with a Kiss (Rachel and John)
Book 2: Playing for Keeps (Sophie and Ryan)
Book 3: Crazy Love (Holly and Daniel)
Book 4: One And Only (Elizabeth and Blake)
Emerald Lake Billionaires: Books 1-3

The Protectors:
Book 1: Safe Haven (Hayley and Tank)
Book 2: Just Breathe (Kelly and Tanner)
Book 3: Always (Mallory and Grant)
Book 4: The Promise (Ashley and Matthew)
The Protectors Boxed Set: Books 1-3

Montana Promises:
Book 1: Coming Home (Mia and Stan)
Book 2: The Gift (Hannah and Brett)
Book 3: The Wish (Claire and Jason)
Book 4: Country Love (Becky and Sean)
Montana Promises Boxed Set: Books 1-3

Sapphire Bay:
Book 1: Falling For You (Natalie and Gabe)
Book 2: Once In A Lifetime (Sam and Caleb)

Book 3: A Christmas Wish (Megan and William)
Book 4: Before Today (Brooke and Levi)
Book 5: The Sweetest Thing (Cassie and Noah)
Book 6: Sweet Surrender (Willow and Zac)
Sapphire Bay Boxed Set: Books 1-3
Sapphire Bay Boxed Set: Books 4-6

Santa's Secret Helpers:

Book 1: Christmas On Main Street (Emma and Jack)
Book 2: Mistletoe Madness (Kylie and Ben)
Book 3: Silver Bells (Bailey and Steven)
Book 4: The Santa Express (Shelley and John)
Book 5: Endless Love (The Jones Family)
Santa's Secret Helpers Boxed Set: Books 1-3

Return To Sapphire Bay:

Book 1: The Lakeside Inn (Penny and Wyatt)
Book 2: Summer At Lakeside (Diana and Ethan)
Book 3: A Lakeside Thanksgiving (Barbara and Theo)
Book 4: Christmas At Lakeside (Katie and Peter)

The Cottages on Anchor Lane:

Book 1: The Flower Cottage (Jackie and Richard)
Book 2: The Starlight Café (Andrea and David)
Book 3: The Cozy Quilt Shop (Shona and Greg)
Book 4: A Stitch in Time (Laura and Joseph)

CHAPTER 1

"*S*amantha Jones?"

She looked up from her desk and smiled. "You can call me Sam."

The man standing in her doorway didn't seem impressed by her friendly welcome. She'd met FBI Special Agent William Parker a couple of times, and at each meeting he was just as formal.

Stepping into her office, he handed her a brown folder. "I have the data you requested on Operation Zeus. The information is confidential and can't leave this office."

"I understand." Sometimes she felt like banging her head against a brick wall. As Technical Development Manager at Fletcher Security, she saw top-secret government reports and military schematics of state-of-the-art weapons all the time. A report describing the security system at a US embassy in Moscow wouldn't tempt her to defect to Russia.

"Did you enjoy the brownies I sent to your office?"

"Ma'am?"

Maybe not. "I sent a box of chocolate brownies to your

field office on Monday. They were to thank your staff for their help with the Munroe case."

"That wasn't necessary, but I'm sure my agents appreciated the gesture. Is there anything else I can help you with?"

"No. I'm happy with the file. I'll call once I'm ready to share my recommendations."

Special Agent Parker nodded. "You know where to find me."

Sam sent him a warm smile. What she got in return was a suspicious stare.

Before she managed to open the folder, her cell phone rang. She half-expected to see her mom's number on the caller display. She'd already missed her dad's birthday because of a project she was working on. If Sam couldn't go to her sister's wedding, she'd be disowned.

Thankfully, the call was from her boss, John Fletcher.

"Can you come and see me?" he asked.

"Sure. I'm on my way." Sam was used to his off-the-cuff meetings. John managed one of the largest high-profile security companies in America. As well as personal protection, they developed and sold some of the most technologically advanced security options on the planet. And Sam was in charge of the team of technicians, physicists, mathematicians, and computer specialists who re-imagined the impossible-to-create products no one had seen before.

Before closing the door, she grabbed a couple of files she wanted to discuss with her boss.

Her personal assistant handed her a piece of paper. "Your mom called. I told her you were in a meeting."

Sam sighed. "Thanks. I owe you."

Hailey smiled. "My thoughtfulness can be repaid with a double-strength cappuccino."

"Done. If Mom calls again, tell her I'll see her tonight. I'm going to see John."

"Okay. Do you want me to reschedule your two o'clock appointment?"

Sam glanced at her watch. Living in Bozeman had definite advantages—especially when it came to the almost nonexistent rush hour traffic. "I should be all right. I'll text you if it looks as though I'll be late."

"Sounds good."

After checking she had everything she needed, Sam headed toward the stairs. As long as John didn't have another project for her team, she would be happy.

SAM KNOCKED on John's office door. "Is it okay if I come in?"

He looked up from behind his huge mahogany desk. "Of course, it is. Thanks for coming to see me on such short notice. Have a seat."

If Sam had to describe her boss in one word, it would be "kind". He genuinely cared about the people he employed and did his best to make sure everyone enjoyed their work.

She sat in one of the chairs opposite his desk. "How can I help you?"

"I have a new project I think you'll be interested in."

Sam's heart sank. Her team was already working at full capacity. If John wanted them to take on another project, something else would have to be put on hold.

"Have you heard of Caleb Andrews?"

She shook her head. "His name isn't familiar. What does he do?"

"He's an IT consultant. Until a year ago he was working in Washington, D.C. When his contract finished, he returned to Montana. He has an issue with a program he's developing."

"And you want my team to look at what he's done?"

"I want *you* to look at what he's done. Do you have the time?"

The main project she was working on was at a critical stage. If she left it to help a new client, she wouldn't meet her tight time frame. "Could another person in my team help him?"

"Caleb is working on a project that involves electromagnetic disturbance. You've worked with the Department of Defense on the Alton satellite project."

This time, Sam's response was more cautious. No one except high-ranking military and government officials knew about her involvement. "That was before I started working here. The Alton project was classified."

"I don't know exactly what you were doing, but it sounds similar to Caleb's project. No one else in your team has the technical or practical experience to help him."

John didn't often ask her to drop everything to assist another client. And when he did, you could guarantee there was a good reason.

Even so, she was still concerned. "EMP is a highly specialized field. Most IT consultants are more focused on general network and program issues."

"Caleb isn't your run-of-the-mill IT consultant."

John's steady gaze told her more about his client than words could have.

Sam worked in an industry that was full of specialists who never talked about their work. Their area of expertise could be so focused it was hard to find anyone who could help them.

"I could ask someone in my team to work on Operation Zeus. Will Mr. Andrews come here or will I meet him somewhere else?"

"At this stage, it's better if you go to him. He's living close to a town called Sapphire Bay. It's on the shore of Flathead Lake. I'll email you his contact information."

"When do you want me to start?"

"Monday morning."

That left two-and-a-half days to bring someone on her team up to speed with her other projects. It wasn't impossible, but both of them would be working through the weekend.

Sam looked at the folders. "I'm assuming Mr. Andrews' project takes precedence over the other work I'm involved with?"

John nodded. "If there's anything that can't wait a week or two, let me know."

"I should be able to reallocate most of my work."

"Thanks, Sam. I appreciate your help."

Sam stood and shook John's hand. "You wouldn't have asked if it wasn't important." As she left his office, she checked the time. She had fifteen minutes to drive across town and talk to a professor about cellular regeneration. If there was one thing she could say about her job—it was never boring.

CALEB WASN'T sure when his life had become so complicated. He'd always been an over-achiever but, even for him, this was ridiculous.

He studied his friend's big, black German Shepherd. "What do you think, Sherlock?"

A deep-bellied sigh filled the office.

Sherlock was as impressed as he was with the progress of his latest project.

Scratch that, Caleb thought. *Lack* of progress would be a better way of describing it. With his fingers tapping on the desk, he tried to figure out what was wrong with the computer program. He'd already gone through each line of code, triple checking the text for errors. Everything made perfect sense, but his program still wasn't working.

By six o'clock, he gave up. His friend, Gabe should be arriving soon. He had driven to Polson to sample wedding cake flavors and look at menu options. It wasn't Caleb's idea of fun, but that's what happened when you were getting married.

A beam of light swung across his office walls.

Sherlock sat to attention.

"Your dad has arrived. Let's go see him." He smiled as Sherlock bolted out of the office. If he ever decided to get a dog, he'd find one like Sherlock. He was intelligent, happy, and loyal—everything Caleb needed when he lived alone in the middle of a forest.

Sherlock patted the front door with his paw.

After peering through the glass side-panel, Caleb flicked open the lock. Gabe was climbing up the veranda stairs. For a man who had been surrounded by wedding options all afternoon, he didn't look too stressed.

Gabe smiled when he saw Sherlock. "Hey, boy. Have you been good?"

Sherlock bounded across the veranda, his tail swishing backward and forward like an out-of-control rotor blade.

"I guess that means you missed me." Gabe gave his dog's back a brisk rub and looked at Caleb. "Was he okay?"

"Apart from chasing a squirrel, he was the perfect canine companion. Did you organize the cake and food?"

"We've narrowed our options down to either vanilla cream or chocolate fudge cake. Dinner is still a work in progress."

Caleb held open the door. "Do you have time for coffee?"

"I thought you'd never ask." Gabe walked through to the

kitchen. "I thought deciding to get married was hard. Planning a wedding is worse."

It didn't seem that long ago that Gabe and his fiancée, Natalie, had stayed here. With a stalker on the loose and Natalie's cottage broken into, Caleb's home had been the perfect hideaway.

"You could always elope," Caleb suggested.

"Natalie's mom wouldn't speak to me if we did that." Gabe opened a cupboard and took out two cups. "It's not so bad. Once we've settled on a menu, we need to find a florist. After that, all we have to do is wait for the wedding. Did you fix the problem you're having?"

Caleb poured coffee into their cups. "Nope. But I took your advice and called Fletcher Security. The owner, John Fletcher, is sending someone from his technical team to help me."

"Can they be trusted?"

"The person he's sending has already worked on a lot of classified projects, so I'm not worried about him seeing what I've done."

"When does he arrive?"

"Monday."

Gabe sipped his coffee. "What's your time frame looking like?"

"The next phase of testing begins in eight weeks. Once I'm over this glitch, I'll have to work fast to get everything ready." Thinking about the million and one things that needed to happen was keeping him awake at night.

"What if you can't make the deadline?"

Caleb sighed. "Then the whole project is put on hold." He took a container of cookies out of his pantry. "If that happens, we'll miss our window in the testing facility. The next available slot is six months away."

"Whatever you're doing must be important."

"It is." Caleb couldn't tell Gabe specific details about the project, but that didn't mean his friend was oblivious to what was happening. He'd seen the long hours Caleb worked and knew how important it was to fix the program. What Gabe didn't know was that the project was part of a much larger Department of Defense program.

"Is there anything I can do?"

"Not unless you can change the weather. I'm hoping we don't get the storm that's supposed to hit. I need Sam's help. If the main road closes, he won't get through."

Gabe helped himself to a cookie. "Fall in Montana can be unpredictable. If it does snow, you might have to use your snowplow again."

In spite of his stress levels, Caleb smiled. "Don't remind me. I must be the only person who's had their plow towed out of a ditch."

"You were lucky you didn't go over the bank."

Caleb picked up his coffee. The same thought plagued him each time he drove along the narrow, winding road. Being miles from the nearest town had its advantages, but it also meant you had to be more self-sufficient—and not do stupid things like drive off the edge of the road.

"I learned my lesson."

"I hope so. If it does snow, you'll be on your own for a few days."

"Not if I can help it." Caleb needed Sam to help find the bug in his program. If that meant hiring a helicopter and flying him here, then that's what he'd do.

The security of the country could depend on it.

SAM OPENED HER PARENTS' front door and sniffed. The smell of chicken, garlic, and fresh herbs wafted toward her. Her mom's pot pies were famous in the Jones' household. And no one, including the prodigal daughter, missed pot pie night.

"Hi, Sam." Bailey, her youngest sister, rushed downstairs. "Mom's in the living room. We're wrapping the table favors."

Sam stepped out of Bailey's way. "I like your hair."

"Thanks." Bailey skidded to a stop, fluffing the curls in her shoulder-length hair. "We had our practice appointment at the Beauty Box today. Tell Shelley her hair looks great. It will make her less grumpy."

"Was Mom happy with how your hairstyles turned out?"

Bailey's smile lifted some of Sam's guilt for not being there. "She was. Don't worry, she wasn't too upset that you had to work."

At least that was one less minefield she had to navigate. The second one wasn't going to be so easy.

"Is that you, Sam?" Her mom's voice drifted into the entranceway.

"It is." Sam shrugged out of her jacket and left it on the coat stand. "I'll be there in a minute."

"The coffeepot's hot."

Bailey waved a roll of navy-blue ribbon in the air. "Shelley's waiting for this. I'll see you in the living room."

With heavy steps, Sam followed her sister. Her mom sat on a chair, cutting a length of tulle into circles. Shelley sat cross-legged on the floor, filling each circle with a bag of candy and tying a ribbon around the top.

"Can I help?"

Shelley wiggled to the right. "Sure. You can help Bailey fill the tulle with candy. She's eating more than she's wrapping."

"I am not. I'm eating the candy from the reject pile."

Sam wondered how a sealed bag of candy could be rejected.

Their mom's eyebrows rose. "Bailey Jones. I swear, if your nose grew any longer you'd look like Pinocchio."

Sam's youngest sister clamped her hand over her nose. She was a bit neurotic about the facial feature she'd inherited from her American-Italian Mom.

"Your nose isn't *that* big," Shelley said unhelpfully.

Twin dots of color appeared on Bailey's cheeks. "Sometimes you can be so mean."

"At least *you're* helping." Shelley turned to Sam. "Why weren't you at the Beauty Box?"

"I had to work."

Shelley wasn't impressed. Somewhere, in all of her twenty-eight years, her sister had forgotten what it was like to focus on something other than herself.

"I'm getting married in two weeks," Shelley reminded them unnecessarily. "You missed our hairdressing appointment *and* our makeup consultation."

Sam sat on the floor beside Bailey. "I told you when you made the appointments that I couldn't leave work early."

Shelley stuck her pixie nose in the air. "Loretta couldn't fit us in any later. She's offered to see you tomorrow at two-thirty."

Their mom handed Sam half a dozen tulle circles. "I'll come with you. And afterward, we'll meet your sisters at Emily's boutique for a final dress fitting."

It was time for Sam to tell them the bad news. "I have to work all weekend." The explosion she was waiting for wasn't far away.

"You can't be serious!" The sparks in Shelley's eyes could have ignited a forest fire. "After all the plans we've made you can't back out now."

"I'm not backing out of anything," Sam said. "We saw Emily two weeks ago. My dress will be perfect and so will yours. Loretta can do whatever she wants with my hair and makeup."

"That's not the point," Shelley screeched. "I'm getting

married. Everything has to be perfect."

"It will be. I'm here now, aren't I?"

Bailey handed Sam a bag of candy. "Shelley's stressed because the florist can't get the peony roses she ordered."

"The theme of the wedding is French country chic. How can you do that without peony roses?" Shelley pushed the party favors she'd wrapped to one side. "I need coffee."

Their mom watched her middle daughter leave the room. "Do you need to work all day, Sam? Just come to the dress fitting."

"It will be fun," Bailey said half-heartedly.

Sam looked closely at her youngest sister. What she really meant was that she needed all the support she could get. At their last fitting, Shelley had been so picky that even their mom lost patience with her.

"What time are you going to the boutique?" Sam asked.

"Four o'clock," her mom replied.

"Say yes," Bailey begged. "It won't be the same without you."

Leaving her youngest sister with Shelley was more than Sam's conscience could handle. By four o'clock, she should have handed over most of her work. Anything that wasn't done would have to wait until Sunday.

"Okay," Sam said. "I'll meet you at Emily's boutique."

Bailey threw her arms around Sam's shoulders. "I knew you wouldn't let us down."

Sam hugged her tight. For most of her life, she'd avoided every frilly, flouncy dress she'd ever seen. But thanks to Shelley, she was walking down the aisle in a dress fit for the ballroom scene in Cinderella. But even though the dress was everything she didn't want, she had other issues. The biggest and worst was the possibility of missing her sister's wedding completely. And if that happened, no one would speak to her again.

CHAPTER 2

*T*he alarm on Caleb's satellite phone blasted through the office. He looked at one of his monitors and saw a silver SUV driving past the security camera. Sam Jones had arrived.

He hoped John's recommendation was as good in real life as he was on paper. It was one thing working with someone in town. It was completely different when his nearest neighbor was a fifteen-minute drive away. If the guy was anti-social, living and working in the same house could be a problem.

Before he opened the front door, Caleb grabbed his jacket. The storm that was supposed to hit Sapphire Bay had changed direction. Instead of two feet of snow, a bitter nor'wester had rattled the shingles on the roof, reminding him about the perils of living in a remote location.

The SUV stopped in front of the garage.

The driver's door opened and Caleb stared at the woman climbing out of the cab. Only a handful of people knew he was living in Sapphire Bay and she wasn't one of them.

Her blue eyes widened as they connected with his. "Hello.

You must be Mr. Andrews. I'm Sam Jones from Fletcher Security."

It wasn't often that he was left speechless. He ran through everything he knew about the person who was supposed to be working with him. None of Fletcher Security's emails had mentioned that Sam was a woman.

"I thought you were a man." Heat rushed to his face. Two seconds ago would have been a good time to think before he opened his mouth.

Sam's smile froze. "Will that be a problem?"

He walked toward her, hoping she didn't think he was a total idiot. "Of course not. Are you happy to stay with me in Sapphire Bay?"

"I've worked in all kinds of locations with clients. If you're worried about my safety, I know how to look after myself."

He wasn't sure whether that was a warning or a statement of fact. Either way, he needed help, and she was his best bet. "You'd better come inside before we both freeze. You can call me Caleb."

Sam opened the passenger door and pulled out two suit-cases. "John said you have a tight deadline for your project."

"I need to finish this phase in the next three weeks." He held out his hand for her bags.

"I can manage. They aren't heavy." She lifted her chin, setting the boundaries to their working relationship.

He shoved his hands into his pockets. He'd always admired people who were independent, but he had a feeling Sam's prickly attitude ran deeper than most.

"Your directions for getting here were really clear."

Caleb wiped his feet on the doormat and opened the front door. "It's easy to get lost if you haven't been here before. John said you live in Bozeman."

Sam nodded. "I grew up there. When Fletcher Security

offered me a job, I couldn't refuse." Her eyes wandered around the entranceway. A smile tugged at her mouth when she saw the moose antler chandelier.

"It was a present from a friend."

"It looks great." She took off her jacket and hung it on the coat stand.

Caleb's eyebrows rose. If she'd worn heavy work boots, black trousers, and a white shirt to make herself look more masculine, she'd failed. Nothing could disguise the soft curves under the starched cotton or the graceful way she walked back to her bags.

He tried to think of something to say, but a big black hole of nothingness replaced his brain.

"I like your house. Did you decorate it yourself?"

"A friend helped me." He picked up one of her suitcases. It was heavier than it looked. "I'll show you where you're sleeping. If you need to use another room for your office, you're more than welcome."

"How many bedrooms do you have?"

"Five." As they climbed the stairs, Caleb pointed to a door on the opposite side of the landing. "My room is over there. You can use the main bathroom. If you need extra pillows or blankets, they're in the linen closet."

When Sam walked into the room he'd chosen for her, she sighed. "This is perfect." Leaving her suitcases on the floor, she walked across to the window.

Pine, spruce, and oak trees surrounded the property. Autumn leaves mixed with evergreens, showcasing Caleb's favorite time of the year. Something about the clean mountain air made him feel alive. Life slowed down and he usually had time to enjoy what nature had created. But this year, he wouldn't be going anywhere until he'd finished his latest project.

He stood beside Sam and pointed into the distance.

"That's Lunar Peak. There's a trail that takes you to the top of the mountain, but I wouldn't try it now. The weather is too unpredictable."

"Thanks for the warning."

The warmth in her eyes stirred something deep inside Caleb. He stepped away, ready to bolt from the room if she looked as though she'd felt the same spark of electricity. "It will probably be snowing in the next couple of weeks. When it does, there are some great ski fields in the area."

"I'm hoping I'm not here long enough to enjoy them." Sam bit her bottom lip. "That didn't come out right, did it?"

It was Caleb's turn to smile. "It's okay. I'm hoping you aren't here that long either. If we can fix my program in the next few days, I'll be the happiest guy in Montana. When you're ready to start work, I'll be downstairs in my office."

"I'll be there soon. I just need to get a few things out of my bag."

Caleb nodded and went downstairs. Working with Sam would be no different than working with anyone else. Hopefully, in less than a week, she'd be back in Bozeman and he'd be moving onto the second phase of his project.

AFTER SAM FOUND the folders she needed, she picked up her laptop and headed downstairs.

It wasn't often that she worked with someone who knew as much as she did about programming. She was looking forward to pitting her mind against Caleb's, tossing ideas around and coming up with a solution to his problem.

Given its location, she'd half-expected Caleb to be living in a bunkhouse or in one of the small vacation cabins dotted around Flathead Lake. But this home was lovelier than most of the homes she'd seen in Bozeman. With its timber walls and sweeping views of the mountains, it reminded her of a secret castle, locked away from the rest of the world. But for all its grandeur, the house still felt warm and cozy.

The house wasn't the only surprise. John hadn't mentioned Caleb's age. With all his work experience she'd expected him to be in his mid-sixties, a little bald, with a tummy that stretched the seams of his shirt.

She couldn't have been more wrong. Caleb Andrews was in his late thirties, had a full head of dark brown hair, and no stretched cotton in sight. And if you added gorgeous blue eyes and a beard that added to his charm, you had a walking, talking, hunk of a man who could tie a woman in knots. But only if a woman wanted to be tied in knots. Which she didn't. Not in the next few years, anyway.

After her sister's excruciating journey to her happy-ever-after, Sam was seriously considering staying single. With that depressing thought in her head, she turned right at the bottom of the stairs and walked along a hallway. The first room she saw was the office. Caleb sat behind a wooden desk, focused on his computer.

"Is it okay if I come in?"

He looked up and smiled. "Of course, it is. How about we head to the kitchen? I can explain what I've been doing while we grab something to drink."

"Sounds good to me." She followed him down the hallway and into the living room. Her eyes widened when she saw the large stone fireplace and the chandeliers hanging from the ceiling. Most of her house would have sat comfortably in this space. "This is beautiful."

"Wait until you see the kitchen. It's my favorite room in the house."

As soon as she stepped through the doorway, Sam knew why. Even though it was a cold, gray day, the kitchen was warm and welcoming. Three pendant lights glowed above the white marble counter. Paintings in rich shades of red, orange, and gold lined the walls. But best of all was the fireplace. Its flames leapt in the grate and the sweet scent of pine filled the kitchen. She could imagine herself sitting in the overstuffed armchair, warming her toes in front of the fire while she worked on Caleb's program.

She walked across to the French doors. A large deck opened onto an equally impressive backyard. "How do you work from your office when you have views like this?"

"Most of the time I work from the kitchen. It's only when things aren't going to plan that I work in my office."

While Caleb turned on the coffeepot, Sam sat on a kitchen stool. "John gave me the background information you provided."

"What do you think?"

"You're ambitious and wouldn't have started the project if you didn't think it would work."

Caleb leaned against the counter. "There are other electromagnetic protection systems available for things like lightning strikes, but they rely on the manufacturer using expensive composite materials."

"Like carbon fibers."

"Exactly. Boeing wants airplanes that give them an edge over their competitors. If their aircraft are less expensive to build, their overhead costs reduce, seats become cheaper, and they make more profit. The aerospace industry also wants cost-effective aircraft that can withstand anything. This software will save companies millions of dollars. They'll be able to use steel in the body of their aircraft instead of carbon fibers. Even the speed of manufacturing will increase."

Sam had been impressed when she read Caleb's report. A program like the one he'd created could change the way people lived. As well as giving manufacturers more choice, it could be the biggest transformation the steel industry had seen in decades.

"Are the steel manufacturers excited?"

Caleb placed a packet of cookies on the counter. "They don't know anything about it."

Sam frowned. "I assumed the main investor in the project would be the steel industry."

"Not this time. Would you like coffee, hot chocolate, or herbal tea?"

"Coffee, please." She studied Caleb as he moved around the kitchen. She knew a diversion tactic when she heard one. But to be fair, whoever was behind the project wasn't her business. "Do you know where your program is failing?"

Caleb opened the refrigerator door. "You don't sugar-coat the truth, do you?"

"You're paying John a lot of money for my time. I wouldn't be here unless you've run out of options."

"Try desperate," Caleb muttered. He filled the cup to the brim and placed it in front of her. "I've gone over the coding so many times, I could repeat it in my sleep."

"We'll go back to basics. You can show me your design document and any brainstorming notes you've kept."

"They're waiting for you in my office."

Sam chose a cookie and picked up her cup of coffee. "As soon as you're ready, we'll get started." Regardless of Caleb's tight time frame, Sam's was worse. Ahead of her were two weekends of wedding-inspired madness. Missing even one day of her sister's schedule wasn't going to happen.

WHILE SAM STUDIED THE WHITEBOARD, Caleb moved a stack of papers off a chair. He wasn't entirely comfortable with her being here. Not because she was a woman, but because he rarely needed help from anyone. And when he did, they never came to his home.

Of all the rooms in his house, the office was his sanctuary. It defined him and kept him on track. Somewhere between the photos on the walls and the framed certificates on his bookcase, he found the motivation to reinvent what everyone else took for granted.

His single-minded determination had given him a life-style he would have envied twenty years ago. His goal had been simple. He wanted a better life than his parents. It wasn't until his mom died that he'd questioned some of the decisions he'd made.

Sam tilted her head sideways. For all his surprise at meeting her, he had to admit that she was better looking than any IT specialist he'd worked with. She was stubborn, too. And if that spark of independence didn't intrigue him, her mind did.

"You have an interesting way of thinking." Her quiet voice cut through the silence in the room.

She was studying the whiteboard, no doubt trying to make sense of the linked concepts. Sam wasn't the first person who had looked at his brainstorming technique and wondered how he solved anything.

"I have a color-coded system. If you see anything in red, it's urgent. Orange is interlinked with other processes or resources, and yellow is important but not essential."

She pointed to a blue line. "What does that mean?"

"It links two unrelated theories."

"Satellites and ocean waves?"

"I have a good imagination." He handed her a folder. If she were as good as John had told him, she'd soon realize what he was doing. "This is the first part of my design document."

Sam took the folder but continued to study the board. "You're interested in simplified pulse waveforms. But why the focus on satellites? If your primary goal is to develop a program that eliminates lightning strikes on aircraft, it wouldn't need to work in outer space." Her eyes widened. "Unless you're planning on disrupting the electromagnetic pulses from satellites or nuclear weapons."

He sat on the edge of his desk, waiting for what she'd say next.

Sam glanced at him before opening the folder. She quickly turned the pages, then finally lifted her eyes. Whether she was shocked or impressed, he couldn't tell.

"An attack on America using electromagnetic pulses will never happen."

He reached for another folder. "Have you heard of Starfish Prime?"

"It was part of a series of high-altitude nuclear tests the Department of Defense carried out in the 1960s. They detonated an atomic bomb above Hawaii. But the damage from the electromagnetic pulse was minimal."

"That's what the government wanted everyone to believe. Look in the folder."

Sam turned to the first page of the report. The executive summary showed just how wrong she'd been. "There were power outages along the West Coast."

"The power grid was immobilized for three minutes. That doesn't sound like a long time, but it was enough to disrupt every commercial and residential property in five states."

Sam knew a large electromagnetic pulse attack would be catastrophic. There would be no more engines.

No more electricity.

No more water.

No more of everything people took for granted.

But there was one thing she didn't understand. "No one reported any problems with the power. Why?"

"The bomb was detonated at eleven o'clock at night.

Everyone was told that maintenance in the sub-stations would cause minor disruptions. Backup generators provided power to hospitals and other commercial businesses."

Sam looked around the office. Apart from the whiteboard, another wall was plastered with notes, photos, and equations. Most people wouldn't see the connection between the different elements, but he was sure she did.

"You really think it's possible to launch a cyber-attack on America?"

"We've already proven it's possible. But until six months ago, the threat was minimal. That changed and the Department of Defense wants a system that will block any EMP attack."

"And your program will do that?"

"When I fix it, it will. The program can be added to any early warning missile system, satellite or, in the case of aircraft, into their flight control systems."

Sam followed one of the color-coded lines on the whiteboard. "It must have taken you months to map out what the program needs to do. Did you design the entire program from here?"

"No. I worked with a group of people in Washington, D.C. After our funding was approved, we split into teams. I'm only responsible for this part of the project."

"Why didn't you ask the other people to help?"

Caleb took a deep breath. "There's been a security breach. I don't know who I can trust."

Sam's eyes narrowed. "What happened?"

"Details about the project were leaked to the media. The Washington PR machine kicked into gear to discredit what was said. But all it takes is for one foreign government to listen, and we could have a major incident on our hands."

"Who's in charge of the project?"

Caleb walked across to the photos on the wall. "This is

Richard Lee, the chairperson of the EMP project. He coordinates the work that's happening around the country."

"Does he know the program isn't working?"

"He knows there's a possibility we won't make the testing facility's time frame."

"He wouldn't have been happy."

"No one will be." Caleb turned away from the photos. "We're working against the clock to bring everything together."

Sam sat on the edge of the chair. "We'd better make a start, then. Can you send me a copy of the program? I'll have a quick look at your coding, then go through everything, line by line."

He didn't bother telling her he'd already gone through the code. She knew as well as he did how easy it was to overlook an error. He just hoped the problem could be fixed in the next three weeks. Otherwise, his reputation and the project's budget would be reduced to a pulp. And that was an outcome he wasn't prepared to accept.

CHAPTER 3

*S*am dropped her glasses onto the desk. With weary hands, she rubbed her eyes, beyond caring about the time. For three days she'd worked beside Caleb, testing, eliminating, and retesting different parts of the program.

Delving into the software was like walking inside a giant maze. But this one was trickier than most.

"I made hot apple cider."

She turned in her chair, smiling gratefully at Caleb. "You must have read my mind."

"It was more like I looked at the time. It's after midnight."

"The bewitching hour." Sam took the cup and sniffed. "It smells delicious."

"The owner of the general store makes his own recipe." The warmth in Caleb's eyes turned to concern. "I appreciate you working day and night to help me, but you need to stop if you get tired."

"We won't isolate the bug unless we check everything. Your fields are correct and the input data isn't corrupted. The issue has to be in the way the different parts of the program interact with each other."

"We can look at that in the morning."

Sam covered an enormous yawn with her hand. "I have to go home this weekend. I'm hoping we'll find the bug before then."

"So am I." Caleb moved some papers off a chair and sat down. "By home, do you mean Bozeman?"

"I do. My sister, Shelley, is getting married next week. Our youngest sister, Bailey, has organized a bachelorette party for this Saturday. I have no idea what we're doing, but it won't be too crazy." The apple cider slid down Sam's throat like nectar. She took another sip, savoring the fruity sweetness.

"Do you like doing crazy things?"

Sam leaned back in her chair. "It depends on your definition of crazy."

Caleb's eyebrows rose.

"I know," she sighed. "I'm a lost cause. If I have to ask you to define 'crazy', then there can't be one spontaneous bone in my body."

"Who told you that?"

"No one. It's obvious. I like plans and lists and triple checking everything. That doesn't leave a lot of room for crazy."

"You'd be surprised. Is the rest of your family like you?"

"We're all different." Sam thought about her lovable, slightly eccentric mother, and her father who would have slept under the stars for six months of the year. "Growing up with an American-Italian Mom and a die-hard cowboy for a Dad made our life interesting."

"How interesting?"

"You'll be bored to tears."

Caleb stretched out his legs. It looked as though he was making himself comfortable for a long story. "Try me."

Just thinking about her mom and dad made her smile.

"Mom's idea of heaven is being in the kitchen, cooking ten different dishes and dispensing advice for lifelong happiness. My dad's life ebbs and flows with the seasons. He was the foreman on a ranch before they moved into town. Now he spends most days in the garden. When he isn't there, he's driving Mom insane with ideas about what he wants to do around the house."

"Sounds like an interesting life. What about your sisters?"

"My sister, Shelley thrives on structure." Sam held her hands four inches apart. "Her wedding planner is this thick. It lists everything she needs to do in one-hour blocks. Bailey is more relaxed."

"Are you the middle daughter?"

"Eldest. I'm thirty-one, Shelley's twenty-eight, and Bailey just turned twenty-six. What about your family?"

Caleb's gaze dropped to his cider. "I grew up in Milwaukee with my mom. I don't have any brothers or sisters."

"Where does your dad live?"

The overhead light cast shadows over the hard planes of his face. "I don't know. I was sixteen when I last saw him."

"That must have been hard," Sam said softly. When Caleb didn't reply, she touched his hand. "What were you like when you were a teenager?"

"I was determined." He lifted his gaze and looked into her eyes. "Mom had three jobs and it still wasn't enough to pay the bills. I wanted more than that. I was lucky." He placed his cup on the table. "We should probably call it a night. Are you happy to start work at eight o'clock tomorrow morning?"

"That's fine."

Caleb moved around the office, closing folders and placing them back on the shelves.

Sam's family had never had a lot of money, but they'd always had each other. Even when her dad's accident had forced him to retire early from the ranch, they'd made the best of what they had and looked after each other. She couldn't imagine not having their support.

She watched Caleb for a few more seconds before picking up their cups. "I'll take these through to the kitchen."

"Thanks. Good night."

Sam hesitated in the doorway. If she didn't say what she was thinking, she might never get the chance again.

Caleb must have sensed that she had something on her mind. He stopped what he was doing and looked at her with a question in his eyes.

"I just wanted to say that you should be proud of what you've achieved. John told me about your career. A lot of people can only dream about the success you've had."

He shrugged and turned off his computer. "Success doesn't make you happy."

"But it can change your life for the better if you want it to. Good night."

"Good night, Sam."

His softly spoken reply made her sigh. He'd done so much with his life—she only hoped that one day he could appreciate just how far he'd come.

THE NEXT MORNING, Caleb increased the pace on the treadmill, pushing himself to complete his run in record time.

Last night, after Sam had gone to bed, he'd stayed awake, thinking about his mom. She'd worked hard to provide for them, to give him the best education and life she could afford. And as long as their dad didn't find them, they were okay.

It wasn't until he was in fourth grade that he realized they were different from other families. The other kids in his class wore newer clothes, they went on all the field trips and had desks full of stationery. He didn't understand the bullying or why his friends abandoned him. But he did understand math and computers, and later, how those two things could transform his life.

Sweat poured off his body. His feet pounded against the belt as he sprinted along the home stretch. In two minutes, he'd cross the finish line, posting his personal best time.

He increased the pace, pumped his arms, and ran hard. The TV screen above him showed crowds of screaming people lining the Champs-Élysées. The black and white checkerboard of the finish line was close. Throwing everything into the last, desperate sprint, he lunged forward, breaking the winner's red tape.

With the roar of the crowd ringing in his ears, he gave a satisfied grunt and moved into cool-down mode.

"Congratulations," Sam said from the doorway.

Caleb jumped and nearly flew off the end of the belt. By the time he found his footing, the treadmill had slowed to an easy jog. He sucked in a lungful of air and tried not to stare at Sam's shorts and baggy T-shirt.

"How long have you been standing there?"

"About five minutes. Can you run in other locations?"

He nodded and concentrated on breathing. A sane man would have pushed aside all thoughts of long legs and sleep-tousled blond hair. But he wasn't sane. He hadn't been since the day Sam stood in his front yard.

She walked across to the stack of towels. "Do you like running?"

"It keeps me focused." Although that focus was being severely tested. Sam moved closer, handing him one of the towels. "Thanks."

She looked at the TV screen.

He brought up the menu, letting the program flick between running locations like a trailer for a travel show. "Which one?"

"Australia. I've always wanted to see the Sydney Opera House."

"Run or walk?"

"Walk. I prefer to run at night."

Caleb's eyebrows rose. He pushed the stop button and rolled to a standstill. "I thought the evenings were reserved for curling in front of the fire with a good book."

Twin spots of color appeared on Sam's cheeks. "Why would you think that?"

He might not have any sisters, but he knew when to tread carefully around a woman—especially when Sam's laser beam stare was cutting him in two. "It's fall. It's cold." He waited for her to let him off the hook. She didn't. "Come on, Sam. I was joking."

The look on her face didn't get any better, but at least her chin dropped back to being semi-annoyed. "I go to the gym four times a week. Sometimes I go bowling with my friends. And when I'm feeling super-social, I go to Charlie's Bar and Grill. What do you do for fun?"

"I sit in front of the fire reading a book." He grinned as he wiped his face with the towel. All things being equal, he thought it was a good time to ignore her full-throttle blush.

"I'm sorry."

Caleb glanced at her before running the towel over the treadmill. "There's nothing to be sorry about."

"Yes, there is. I was rude. It doesn't matter what either of us does in our spare time."

"I agree." He moved away and Sam stepped onto the treadmill.

"I mean, so what if my sister thinks I'll be an old maid? It's none of her business what I do." She frowned at the control panel.

Caleb leaned across the hand grips and pointed to a button. "Push this to start. The arrows beside it set the incline, speed, and distance. The emergency stop is here. Cool-down kicks in automatically when you've finished. I take it you're talking about Shelley?"

Sam pushed the start button. "Ever since Jarrod stuck a ring on her finger, she's made everyone's life difficult."

"Maybe she wants you to be as happy as she is?"

"That's the thing. I don't know if she *is* happy." Sam increased the speed. "Whenever Shelley gets stressed, she gets bossy. Mom and Bailey try to keep out of her way, but it's not easy when they live around the corner from each other."

"Have you talked to her?"

Sam frowned. "It wouldn't do any good. Shelley never listens to anything I say."

Caleb moved across to a yoga mat. If he didn't start stretching, he'd be hobbling around the house like an old man. "At least you have sisters. It's worse when you don't have anyone to talk to."

"Who do you talk to when you're worried?"

He stretched his right leg, wishing he hadn't said anything. "Friends."

"Do they help?"

"Sometimes." He closed his eyes and focused on the pull of his muscles.

"She's right."

Caleb opened his eyes. "Who's right?"

"Shelley."

He wound back their conversation and tried to figure out what she meant. "You're too young to be an old maid."

"It's not funny," Sam muttered.

"I didn't say it was."

"You're smiling. Smiling means you find it amusing."

"I find it...interesting."

Sam held her finger on the speed button. "I've changed my mind. I need to run."

Appreciating the sight of her long legs speeding along the treadmill wouldn't get the kinks out of his body—it would only create more. With a resigned sigh, he stretched his other leg.

"We should talk about the project," Sam said. "I was thinking about the stack trace."

Caleb was thinking about a whole lot of other things. Things that could get him into serious trouble.

"At the point where the program failed, eight major functions were being initiated. We've tested four and they seem okay."

Sam was barely out of breath. Her sessions at the gym must have been more intense than Caleb thought.

"The core dump gave us a snapshot of what was happening when the program crashed. If we compare that to the stack trace, then cross-reference it to the four remaining functions, we might be able to isolate the bug."

"Does your brain ever switch off?"

Sam wiped her forehead and grinned. "Not usually. Dad says it's one of my more endearing qualities."

"You should listen to him instead of your sister."

"That's what Mom said—after she told me she's looking forward to cuddling her grandbabies."

He walked across to the clean towels and grabbed one for Sam. "It sounds like you'll never win."

"I don't need to," she muttered. "After Shelley gets married, everything will go back to normal." With one last jab at the control panel, she ran toward the Sydney Opera House.

He was glad Sam felt optimistic because, from where he was standing, it didn't sound as though anyone's life would be the same again. Between wedding vows and babies, Sam's single days might be numbered. Especially if her sister and mom had anything to say about it.

ON SATURDAY MORNING, Sam stood behind Caleb's chair, nibbling on a fingernail. "How does it look?"

"About the same as the last time you asked."

She squinted at the screen. "If it was going to fail, it would have done it by now."

Caleb leaned forward, staring at the color-coded outputs appearing on his screen. "The third phase is complete."

Sam held her breath as another function reached eighty percent completion. She glanced at her watch, surprised that it was nearly lunchtime. They'd been working since six o'clock this morning, cross-checking everything before their first trial run.

"The fourth phase is complete." Caleb tapped his fingers against the desk.

The next set of processes was crucial. Yesterday afternoon they'd found a bug in a sub-processor. They had no idea if fixing it would create another problem—but they were about to find out.

Sam walked across to the window and stared at the leaves scattered across the yard.

"Fifth phase complete."

She bit her bottom lip. If the next three functions worked, she could go home, surround herself with satin and tulle, and be the maid of honor her sister wanted.

The tapping of keys had her spinning around. "What is it?"

With his head bent over his keyboard, Caleb's entire focus was on his computer.

She ran across the room and peered over his shoulder. "Something happened during the sixth phase."

"Is it related to the bug we found yesterday?"

Caleb sighed as he aborted the program. "I don't know. We'll do another core dump and see what happened."

"At least we made it to the sixth phase." Even to Sam's ears, her positive spin on today's test sounded weak. "It could be worse."

"Not much." He didn't move.

Even after working until midnight most nights, Caleb hadn't looked so exhausted or seemed so defeated.

"Come on." Sam spun his chair around. "We've both been working long hours. And even if you aren't hungry, I am. How about we have some lunch before we look at the program again?"

Caleb ran his hands through his hair. "I have a better idea. I need more groceries and you need to drive back to Bozeman. We can have lunch in Sapphire Bay, then go our separate ways after that."

"I can't leave now. The program isn't working."

"Your sister has organized a bachelorette party. Unless you want to be banned from the wedding, you have to be there."

Sam's eyes widened. "I never thought of that. I wouldn't have to wear the frilly dress Shelley chose or sit for hours while Loretta does my hair and makeup."

"You also won't be part of the most important day of your sister's life. You're driving to Bozeman."

"Have I told you how annoying you can be?"

Caleb laughed. "Not since yesterday."

His smile made Sam's tummy spin in cartwheels. Caleb Andrews was too much of a distraction, and that was the last thing she needed. She cleared her throat and pointed to his computer. "You should start the next core dump."

Caleb tilted his head to the side. "Yes, ma'am."

She waited for him to move, but he stayed exactly where he was, staring into her eyes. If she thought his smile made her feel off-center, the warmth in his gaze made her feel more unsettled.

"Caleb?"

"Yes?"

"Start the core dump." The huskiness in her voice made her cringe. Caleb was a client of Fletcher Security. Feeling anything other than professional respect was out of the question. *Way* out of the question.

Caleb's slow smile made her blush. It was just as well this assignment was nearly finished.

"You're impossible," she muttered as she walked across to the doorway. "I'll meet you by the entranceway in ten minutes."

"Pack for the weekend. I don't want to see you back here until Monday morning."

"Sunday night," she said over her shoulder. "We need to fix your program." Unless he did that when she wasn't here. Her heart sank. If that happened, she might not see him again.

As they left the café, Caleb held open the door for Sam. Coming to Sapphire Bay for lunch was the best idea he'd had all week. Over grilled sandwiches and coffee, they'd talked about their work, the things that were important to them, and the things they'd sooner forget.

As soon as she stepped onto the pavement, Sam zipped up her jacket and pulled on a bright blue, wooly hat. "I want to visit the candy store before I head home. Thank you for a lovely lunch."

He looked into Sam's upturned face and took a deep breath. She really was the most stunning woman he'd ever met. "I can walk with you. The general store is a couple of doors down from Brooke's candy store."

"You know the owner?"

"I met her not long after I moved to Sapphire Bay. She worked from her converted garage for eighteen months before opening the store." Caleb glanced at Sam, hoping she didn't think anything romantic had happened between him and Brooke.

"I've already been in her store. I bought some fudge on my way to your house. It was incredible."

Caleb knew how good Brooke's candy tasted, and so did most of Sapphire Bay. He pointed down the street. "There's a line out the door."

Sam's eyes widened. "I didn't know her store was that popular."

"It's Saturday. She used to go to the market to sell her candy but, as soon as she opened the store, she couldn't keep up with the demand." He stood at the end of the line and peered through the large glass windows. Brooke was behind the counter with Kathleen Armstrong, serving their customers.

Caleb hadn't seen Kathleen or her daughter, Natalie, for a couple of weeks. If his best friend, Gabe hadn't come out to his property, he wouldn't have seen him either.

They slowly moved forward. The smell of rich chocolate tickled Caleb's nose. He didn't usually have a sweet tooth, but he was addicted to Brooke's fudge. "I've been trying to convince Brooke to start an online store. It would take some of the foot traffic away and increase her revenue."

"I guess it takes time to set up everything."

Caleb stepped closer to the front counter. "That's what Brooke said. At the moment, the store's so busy that she doesn't have time to do anything except create more candy. What are you going to buy?"

"Mom loves fudge, so I'll get her a selection of flavors. Dad likes sucking on rock candy, so I'll buy him some of the raspberry whopper sticks I saw on Monday. Bailey will enjoy the sherbet, and Shelley isn't eating anything except lettuce leaves, so I'll buy her some Russian fudge to annoy her."

"I'm sure everyone, except Shelley, will be suitably impressed."

Sam grinned. "So am I."

Caleb knew he didn't have to wait in line with Sam, but he wanted to delay the moment when he said goodbye. If that made him desperate, he didn't care. He liked her company and wouldn't be this far through debugging his program without her. And besides, there were worse things he could be doing than standing in a candy store.

"Caleb!" Brooke's warm smile made him glad he was here. "I thought you were hiding in your house for a few weeks."

"I've run out of food. Brooke, this is Sam Jones. Sam's working on a project with me."

Brooke held out her hand. "Hi, Sam. It's nice to meet you. I hope Caleb isn't working you too hard."

Sam's quick smile made him sigh.

"He's okay. I've had worse clients."

Caleb's eyebrows rose. "Hey, I'm standing right here."

"Don't worry," Brooke said. "I know what Sam means. You can have a one-track mind sometimes. Do you want to know the secret to Caleb's happiness, Sam?"

Sam glanced at him and grinned. "It might come in handy."

"Caramel fudge. If he gets grumpy, hand him a bar and see what happens."

Caleb frowned. Brooke made him sound like one of the seven dwarfs. "I'm not that bad."

Sam and Brooke looked at each other and smiled.

"Only sometimes," Brooke added. "What can I get you?"

Sam studied the cabinet in front of them. "I'll start with a box of caramel fudge."

Caleb groaned. Sam was taking Brooke's advice seriously. It was true—he really did have a thing for her fudge. But it wasn't the secret to his happiness. That had arrived in a five-foot-eight body with blond hair and sparkling blue eyes. And to make matters worse, he was worried his addiction to Sam might be worse than the candy.

CHAPTER 4

*S*am parked her truck in her parents' driveway. She had no idea what Bailey had planned for their sister's bachelorette party, but she hoped it wasn't too wild. Shelley was already worried about the wedding. Taking her to a noisy, over-the-top party would make everything worse.

Leaves crunched under her boots as she walked across the front yard. Her parents' two-story house wasn't as large or as grand as Caleb's, but just looking at it made her feel warm and cozy.

When her parents moved into town, it was a big deal, especially for her dad. Ranching was his life. He lived and breathed the open spaces, the sound and smell of the cattle, and the natural rhythm to life. He'd never owned a property in town and it took more than a few months for him to feel as though he belonged. But looking back, it was the best thing her parents could have done.

Sam opened the front door. "Anyone home?" she yelled into the entranceway.

"We're in the kitchen," her mom yelled back.

Leaving her suitcase beside the hall table, Sam made her way through the house.

"You made it." Her mom, Elena, wrapped her in a hug.

"The roads were better than I thought." She took off her jacket and smiled at her parents. "What are you doing?" Her great-grandmother's silver cutlery was spread across the table.

Ted, Sam's dad, placed a freshly polished knife on the table. "Your mom has invited half her family to stay with us after the wedding. We're getting the silver ready for inspection."

Elena swatted her husband's arm with the polishing cloth. "I only invited my sisters."

"And their families," he mumbled.

Sam laughed. "Let me guess—Aunt Rosa and Aunt Maria?"

"They're coming a long way for the wedding. It would be a shame not to make the most of their visit."

Ted looked over the rim of his glasses. "They live in San Francisco and, if I'm not mistaken, they were here four months ago."

Elena's shoulders lifted in a very Italian shrug. "Family is family. You should be thankful my brothers decided to stay in a hotel."

Her dad picked up a fork and kept polishing. "I'll be forever grateful."

Sam grinned at her parents. The Italian side of their family was loud, boisterous, and lots of fun. And, contrary to what her dad had said, he enjoyed their company—especially when they took over the kitchen.

Her mom left her cloth on the table and studied Sam. "You're getting skinny. Are you eating enough?"

"I'm eating plenty."

Her mom didn't look as though she believed her. "I have

toasted ravioli in the oven. A little salsa and salad and you have a meal fit for a king."

If Sam didn't find her sisters soon, she'd end up spending the rest of the night eating. "I really am okay. The client I'm working with bought me lunch."

"Lunch was hours ago. You need food to give you energy. Sit with your father while I bring you a little something."

Her dad pulled out the chair beside him. "Let your mom spoil you. You've been away a lot over the last few weeks."

Sam sank into the chair. When she wasn't working in Bozeman, she was careful about what she told her family and friends. Most of the work she did was confidential. If anyone discovered the names of the clients she worked with, Fletcher Security's reputation would be in shreds.

"Can you tell me what you've been doing?" her dad asked.

Sam shook her head.

"What about the client who bought you lunch? Do they have a name?"

"They do, but I can't tell you who he is."

Her mom turned around. "You're working with a man? Is he nice?"

Sam leaned her elbows on the table. If she didn't change the subject, her mom would keep asking questions. "He's a good man. Are Bailey and Shelley here?"

"They're upstairs getting ready. Shelley's friends are arriving in an hour." Her mom opened the oven door. "A good man is worth one hundred of those flashy types. Your father is a good man. That's why I married him."

Ted winked at Sam. "I thought it was because I was handsome."

"That, too," Elena said. "Your good man wouldn't happen to be single and Italian, would he?"

If Sam weren't so tired, she would have smiled. But after

working until midnight most nights this week, she was exhausted. "I'm not going to marry him, Mom."

"It doesn't hurt to keep your options open."

Ted patted her hand. "Your mom means well."

"I know," Sam whispered. She glanced at her watch. "I really need to see Shelley and Bailey."

"Your ravioli will be here when you come downstairs," her mom said as Sam left the kitchen. "And tell your sisters they'll need to eat something before they leave, too."

"I'll tell them."

"I love you."

Her mom's voice followed Sam into the hallway. After spending a lot of time away from her family, it was good to hear those words. Because regardless of how much money you earn or where you come from, everyone should know they are loved.

SAM OPENED the bedroom door at the end of the landing. Her sisters should be getting ready for a bachelorette party, not Halloween. "Why are you wearing black-and-white striped coveralls?"

Shelley threw her hands in the air. "I told you no one would know we're prisoners. We look like we belong in a horror movie."

Sam was still confused. "What do prisoners have to do with a bachelorette party?"

Bailey added a coat of peach lip gloss to her mouth. "The Museum of the Rockies is having their annual fundraiser. This year, they've organized a Murder in the Museum night. I thought it would be fun to go along."

Shelley sat on the end of the bed. "We have to look for clues and find a killer."

"Oh." Sam studied Shelley's face. "I take it this isn't where you would have chosen to have your bachelorette party?"

Bailey threw a pair of coveralls at Sam. "Shelley had a list of ridiculous requirements for her party. The museum event met most of them, except the dead body part. That was a happy coincidence."

"There's nothing happy about it," Shelley groaned. "No one goes to a bachelorette party at the museum."

"Think of it this way…" Bailey looked as though she was about to put every last ounce of her psychology degree to good use. "…apart from supporting a good cause, your friends won't have done this before. By lunchtime tomorrow, your bachelorette party will be the talk of the town."

Sam pulled on the coveralls. "At least it's better than standing in a noisy bar, drinking margaritas and French champagne."

"I'll take the French champagne any day." Shelley studied her reflection in the full-length mirror. "How do I look?"

Sam sent Bailey a warning glance. Knowing her youngest sister, she'd say something funny, and Shelley would take it the wrong way.

"You look beautiful," Bailey said.

The front doorbell rang. Shelley pulled back the curtains and looked into the front yard. "My friends are here."

Bailey handed her a tiara with a scrap of lace attached to the back. "Wear this. It will look cute with your costume."

Shelley jammed the tiara onto her head and ran out of the room.

"How did you convince her to wear the coveralls?" Sam asked.

"She didn't have a choice. I'd already bought the tickets and sent everyone their costumes. Our team is called the Jail House Brides. It's going to be an awesome night."

A few minutes later, Sam knew Bailey was right. No one would forget Shelley's bachelorette party.

Downstairs, nibbling on her mom's toasted ravioli, were six excited women all dressed in black and white striped coveralls. She didn't know what Caleb was doing tonight, but it couldn't top where she was going.

Especially if they found the murderer.

~

CALEB STRETCHED his legs in front of him. Gabe had invited him for dinner and Natalie, Gabe's fiancée, had joined them.

In the two years since he'd met Gabe, Caleb had never seen him so happy. The former NYPD detective, turned New York Times bestselling crime writer, was working on his fourth novel and getting ready for a whirlwind book tour.

"I still think we should stay in New Orleans for another week," Natalie said. "Just think of all the research you could do."

"I need to be back in Manhattan for the twentieth," Gabe reminded her. "We could stay for two days, but no more."

"Take the two days," Caleb said to Natalie. "You'll have a great time."

"Have you been to New Orleans?"

"A couple of times. Be careful around the mounted police. Their horses move fast."

"Another friend said the same thing." Natalie picked up Gabe's itinerary. "Okay. Two days it is. This could be the closest we get to a vacation until our honeymoon."

The smile that Gabe sent his fiancée made Caleb wish for a whole lot of things that might never happen.

"I'll make everyone a cup of coffee," Natalie said as she handed Gabe his itinerary. "Don't make any plans while I'm gone."

Caleb waited until Natalie was out of the room before speaking to his friend. "Does she know where you're taking her for your honeymoon?"

"Not yet. I thought I'd surprise her."

Caleb nodded. The Pacific Island honeymoon Gabe had booked didn't require extra packing or special equipment. All they'd need was a swimsuit and a bottle of sunscreen.

"Is everything all right?" Gabe leaned forward. "You're quieter than usual."

"It's been a long week."

"Is your program working?"

Caleb thought about the hours he'd spent with Sam. If it weren't for her quirky sense of humor and endless energy, he wouldn't be feeling optimistic about fixing the program. "It's not working yet. Sam's a big help, but we can't find what's wrong."

"You should have brought him with you. Having some down time can help your brain process information differently."

"Sam went home for the weekend. And she's a woman, not a man."

Gabe's eyebrows rose. "When did that happen?"

Caleb smiled. "At a guess, I'd say it was before she was born."

"Very funny." Gabe tilted his head to the side. "Tell me about her."

"You can't include her in one of your books."

"Would I do that?"

"In a heartbeat," Caleb muttered. Gabe's thirst for new and interesting characters was matched by a keen intelligence. He enjoyed dissecting a person's personality, waving it like a red flag in front of his imagination, and seeing what happened.

Gabe sat back in his chair. "Let me guess. Her IT skills

came highly recommended, so she must be good. She'd need a logical mind and a lot of courage to rise through a male-dominated profession. I'm assuming she shortened her name to add to the persona she's created. University educated, some private high-powered contract work. Thirty something. Single. Not interested in mixing her professional and personal life. How am I going?"

Caleb was shocked at Gabe's accuracy. "You're showing off."

Natalie carried a tray of hot drinks into the living room. "That's Gabe for you."

Gabe grinned at his fiancée. "Years of profiling with the NYPD comes in handy."

"Who were you talking about?"

"An IT specialist. She's staying with Caleb."

Natalie handed Caleb a cup of coffee. "How close was Gabe to describing her?"

Closer than Caleb was comfortable with. "Fairly accurate."

"What's she really like?"

If Sam knew they were talking about her she wouldn't return to Sapphire Bay. "She's...interesting."

Gabe choked on his coffee.

Natalie sent her fiancé a withering glance. She turned back to Caleb, ignoring Gabe's coughing fit. "What does she like doing when she's not working with computers?"

An image of Sam running on the treadmill filled his mind. She was the cutest IT manager he'd ever met. "She runs, goes to the gym, and spends time with her friends. Where are you up to with your wedding?"

"I'm meeting with the florist next Wednesday."

As Natalie told him about their latest wedding drama, Caleb looked at Gabe—and wished he hadn't. It was bad enough that he couldn't stop thinking about Sam; worse that his closest friend could see straight through him.

After spending five days with Sam, he knew he was in trouble. Falling for the Technical Development Manager at Fletcher Security wasn't part of his plans. Even if she could look after herself.

~

"LOOK UNDER THE WAGON," Bailey whispered. "It has to be here somewhere."

Sam glanced over her shoulder before crawling under the barrier rope. "I'm not supposed to be here."

"Don't worry. No one can see you."

That was easy for Bailey to say. She wasn't the person scanning the bottom of a wagon that was covered in more than one hundred years of dirt and dust. Sam coughed as she pulled out her cell phone. The flashlight lit the underside of the wagon like fireworks exploding in the night sky. This was almost the craziest thing they'd done all night. But top prize went to climbing over the glass balustrade that kept everyone away from Big Mike, the T-Rex dinosaur skeleton in the lobby.

If it weren't for Shelley's quick thinking, they would have ended up on the ten o'clock news, surrounded by an avalanche of dinosaur bones and a very unhappy museum director.

"Hurry up," Bailey hissed. "We won't be able to keep the other teams away for much longer."

"I'm going as fast as I can." Sam slid farther under the wagon. Part of her was impressed with the workmanship that had created the rough and rugged vehicle. The other part wanted to find the missing clue and get out of here fast.

A glimmer of white flashed against the dark, dented

wood. She wiggled closer, shining the flashlight higher. Bingo! "I've found it." She grabbed the piece of paper and crawled backward. "Text everyone and tell them we're on the move."

"It's too late."

"What do you mean?" By the time Sam crawled clear of the wheels, three pairs of glittering red shoes were lined up beside Bailey's feet.

Sam dropped her head to her chest. The Wizard of Oz team had found them. But they hadn't found the clue.

For the first time all night, she was thankful the sleeves of her coverall were too long. The cotton hung over her hands and for a few minutes, would camouflage the small piece of paper she'd shoved under the stretchy wristband of her watch.

She clambered to her feet, blowing a stray strand of hair off her face. "Hi."

A woman Sam had met earlier, smiled. "Did you find the clue?"

"I thought I had, but it was an old receipt. The wheel of the wagon must have picked it up the last time it was outside." After six years in the Army, countless private security operations, and growing up with two sisters, her ability to stretch the truth was outstanding. And one day, it would get her into trouble.

The smile on the woman's face dimmed. "Are you sure?"

"You can look if you like. It's above the right-hand wheel at the back of the wagon."

The three women knelt on the wooden floor, staring under the wagon.

"It's over there," Sam pointed to the far side of the exhibit. She caught Bailey's gaze and nodded toward the main doors of the exhibition space.

Without second-guessing herself, she grabbed her sister's

hand and ran across the room. "Where's the rest of our team?"

"They should be in the lobby."

Shelley was the first person they saw.

"Quick," Sam said as she slowed to a walk. "Come with us."

Everyone followed them into the nearest bathroom.

Bailey checked under the cubicle doors. "Clear."

"Are you sure you don't work for the government?" Sam joked.

"I've watched too many TV programs. Where's the clue?"

The team huddled around Sam as she read the slip of paper. "The first five words of Lewis Carroll's *Jabberwocky* reveal Professor MacIntosh's murderer. When you have your answer, stand in the middle of the Taylor Planetarium and see what happens."

Shelley held out her cell phone. "I've got it. The first five words of the poem are, 'Twas brillig, and the slithy'. What does that mean?"

"There are no characters called brillig or slithy," Bailey said.

When no one else realized what they were looking at, Sam gave them a clue. "It's an acronym."

"What's an acronym?" Bailey asked.

Sometimes Sam couldn't believe her sister had spent five years at college. "It's when the first letter of a word forms part of another word."

"Twas Bats!" Shelley shrieked.

"Ssh!" Bailey hissed. "We don't want the other teams to hear the answer."

While everyone was congratulating Shelley on her powers of deduction, Sam opened the bathroom door. Bats, Professor MacIntosh's petite personal assistant, stood beside a large Grecian urn. If Sam had to choose a murderer, Bats was the last person she would have picked. She had a good alibi and an even better reason why she wouldn't have killed her boss. Or so Sam had thought.

Instead of focusing on the redhead who'd fooled them all, she studied the other people in the atrium.

"What are you looking at?" Bailey asked.

Sam closed the door. "The Wizard of Oz team is heading toward the planetarium. Do you think they know who murdered Professor MacIntosh?"

"I doubt it. They're probably looking for us."

"We need to get there first," Shelley whispered.

For someone who hadn't wanted to wear striped coveralls, Shelley had quickly dropped into super sleuth mode.

"What are you suggesting?" Bailey asked.

"We run. They're wearing high heels. We're in sneakers. We can beat them to the planetarium."

Everyone in their team nodded their agreement. Shelley led the charge, followed closely by Bailey. With more speed than finesse, their team raced across the lobby, stopping in the center of the planetarium before anyone knew what they were doing.

With eyes wide open, Shelley spun in a slow circle, studying the rows of seats stacked one behind each other. "What now?"

Mr. Quirk, the person Sam had decided was the most likely to be the murderer, walked toward them.

"May I help you…ladies."

The sneer in his voice made Sam bristle.

Shelley stepped forward. "We know who killed Professor MacIntosh."

He coughed delicately into his gloved hand. "Really?"

Sam frowned. Either the guy was a good actor or sarcasm came easily to him. If he thought being high-handed around

Shelley would make his job easier, he was in for a rude awakening.

"Yes. Really." Shelley's chin rose a few degrees. "We've solved the final clue."

"You have? How delightful."

Sam handed her sister the piece of paper.

Shelley cleared her throat. Most of the teams were making their way into the planetarium. "The first five words in Lewis Carroll's *Jabberwocky* poem spell the murderer's name." She waited for a few seconds, controlling the anticipation in the room with the skill of a diplomat. "The person who murdered Professor MacIntosh is Bats."

A gasp rang out from the crowd of super-sleuths.

Bats stepped forward. "It's lies, all lies," she shrieked.

Sam looked at their team. Half of Shelley's friends were in a state of shock, the other half was enjoying every minute of the spectacle they were creating.

Bat's hand shook as she pointed to Shelley. "You don't know what you're talking about. Show me your evidence."

Instead of looking as bemused as Bailey, Shelley straightened her shoulders and took a deep breath. She wasn't chosen as the lead role in three consecutive high school plays for nothing. If anyone could pull off a dramatic conclusion to tonight's fundraiser, it was Shelley.

As she launched into a dazzling performance, Sam proudly watched the admiration on the faces of the people around them. Even Mr. Quirk rubbed his hands together, no doubt waiting for his moment to shine in the volley of accusations being hurled around the room.

"Look at the other teams," Bailey whispered to Sam. "They're loving every minute of this."

"The organizers couldn't have planned the ending any better if they'd tried."

Shelley concluded her speech by thrusting the final clue under Mr. Quirk's long, pointy nose.

The audience clapped and cheered when Charlie Chaplin, dressed as a police officer, arrived center stage to arrest Bats.

Ten minutes later, Shelley accepted the winning prize on behalf of their team. She waved the trophy high in the air before handing it to her teammates. It was a night no one would forget, least of all the bride-to-be. Shelley looked happier than she had for a long time.

Now all they had to do was keep her smiling.

CHAPTER 5

*C*aleb glanced at his watch. Sam had called an hour ago to say she'd arrived in Sapphire Bay. Even with the snow that had fallen earlier in the day, she should be here by now.

He sent her another text from his satellite phone. If she didn't pull into the garage soon, he would head outside and look for her. The roads could be dangerous at any time, but as fall turned into winter, they became worse.

To take his mind off Sam, he opened the latest program report. After he'd driven home last night, he'd run a different debugging scenario. He'd prayed for a miraculous cure to his coding woes but, as usual, the program had stopped before the first series of functions was complete.

He ran his eye across the first line of code, then the second. A few minutes later, he looked at his phone. Still no word from Sam.

This was ridiculous. Her truck could have hit black ice and skidded off the road. Or she might have underestimated the amount of gas in her tank. Caleb grabbed his jacket and walked into the garage. He checked his truck. Spare chains, a first-aid kit, and extra blankets. A can of gas wouldn't go amiss, either. When he was ready, he opened the garage door and felt the icy blast of the sub-zero temperature.

If Sam had abandoned her truck, she'd have hypothermia before she found help.

The deep bellow of a foghorn erupted from his phone. He checked the security app and sighed. Sam's truck had activated the camera on his front gate. He'd never been more grateful for anything in his life.

He rested his head against the driver's door and took a deep breath. She was okay. No one had hurt her. She hadn't driven off the road or had an accident.

Sam's headlights lit the garage. She parked beside his truck and waved. "Hi."

His heart squeezed tight. "Hi. I was about to look for you. I thought you must have had an accident."

Sam closed the driver's door and sighed. "It was a slow drive. There was a slip on the main road and traffic is down to one lane. The Highway Patrol is trying to keep everyone moving, but there's a big line of trucks waiting to get through. I tried calling you, but there was no signal."

He closed the garage door and took Sam's bag out of her hand. "A normal cell phone doesn't work that well out here. I'll lend you a satellite phone. Would you like a hot drink?"

"That would be great. What have you been doing?" Sam pulled off her red wooly hat and unzipped her jacket.

Thank goodness she didn't realize how worried he'd been. "I had dinner with two friends last night. Gabe and Natalie said hello."

"Do they live nearby?"

"They're in Sapphire Bay." As they walked into the hallway, Caleb had to stop himself from reaching out and holding her hand. Sam had only been gone a day, but the house had felt empty without her.

Two weeks ago, he wouldn't have traded his life for anything. He had good friends and a job he loved. His home wasn't the rustic hideaway some people craved—he had too many gadgets and high-end security options for that—but living this close to nature refueled him and made him appreciate life more than he ever had.

But as he listened to Sam telling him about her sisters, it made him more aware of what was missing from his life. Family. A soft place to fall. Someone who accepted him warts and all. He'd never had any of that and there was a strong chance he never would.

"When Charlie Chaplin handcuffed Bats, everyone in the planetarium began cheering. The museum director said it was the best fundraiser they'd had in years."

Caleb walked into the kitchen and turned on the coffeepot. "Did you take any photos?"

Sam pulled out her cell phone. "What you're about to see isn't your run-of-the-mill Murder in the Museum night."

Nothing Sam did would ever be ordinary. "I consider myself warned."

"Okay, here goes."

He sat beside her, looking forward to seeing what she'd been doing.

"Exhibit one—our coveralls. They aren't glamorous, but they were perfect. Bailey ordered them from an online costume store."

"I like the stripes."

"Jailbird chic." Sam flicked to the next photo. "That's Bats. No one suspected she was the murderer. Look at those big blue eyes. Is that the face of someone who would shoot Professor MacIntosh in the back?"

"I can see how you were fooled." Or maybe not. Apart from not meeting any murderers before, Caleb wasn't in a fit state to pass judgment on anyone. His brain was seriously dysfunctional—not because of the long hours he'd been working, but because of Sam.

She was so close that he could smell the light floral scent of her perfume, feel the movement of air as she laughed at the next photo. Instead of moving away, he angled his body closer—wanting to be part of the excitement that lit her face.

The next photos showed other teams in the fundraiser, the murder weapon, and one of Shelley's friends lying in the yellow outline of the victim's body.

"This is a photo of our team." Sam tapped the screen. "Everyone went back to Mom and Dad's house to show them our trophies." Sam's smile was replaced by a frown. "I haven't seen Shelley so happy in a long time."

"That's a good thing, isn't it?"

"I'm not sure. She's usually so calm. Her mood has been swinging up and down so much that I don't know if she remembers what normal feels like."

"It's probably wedding jitters. Gabe and Natalie are organizing their wedding, too. It's not easy balancing what each of you wants for your big day."

"I hope that's all it is." She handed Caleb her phone. "This is a picture of Mom, Dad, and my sisters. A friend of Bailey's took the picture this morning."

Caleb was surprised at how different Sam looked from the rest of her family.

"I wasn't adopted, if that's what you're thinking. Shelley and Bailey take after mom's Italian heritage. Dark hair, brown eyes and a little on the short side. I'm more of a Jones, although Dad is more gray than blond." She smiled at Caleb. "He says that's what he gets for raising three daughters."

"It couldn't have been all hard work."

"I don't think so, but Dad might not agree. Have you worked on the program today?"

"I did. It's still aborting." He took two cups out of the

cupboard. "If you want to look at the latest debugging stats, they're on my desk. I'll bring our coffee in when it's ready."

Sam slipped off the stool. "Mom made us chocolate chip cookies. We can have some with our drinks." She opened her bag and pulled out an orange container. "I'll see you in the office."

Caleb poured hot coffee into their cups. At some point in the next few days, Sam would go home. The program would be working and he'd have more time to focus on the next phase of the project.

Whether he could forget about her was a different issue, and more difficult than any software problem he'd had to fix.

CALEB STOOD in his office doorway. Sam sat cross-legged in an armchair, studying one of the folders he'd left on his desk. "What do you think?"

She looked up. Surprise, shock, and something far deeper left her skin pale and her eyes as dark as a winter's storm. "When were you going to tell me?"

"What are you talking about?" He walked into the office, placing the two cups on his desk.

Sam held up a pale blue folder.

He held his breath. No one would blame her for being upset. He'd felt sucker-punched, too, when he'd read the contents of the folder. "I'm sorry. You weren't supposed to see that."

Sam stared, open-mouthed at him. "Someone wants to kill you, and you didn't tell me?"

"The Al-Nusra Nuclei is a radical terrorist group. They make death threats all the time."

"And you didn't think it was important enough to tell anyone?"

He winced. What he said next wouldn't make any difference to her reaction, but it might explain why he hadn't said anything. "It's not me the Al-Nusra want, it's my program. As soon as the Department of Defense has it, they'll leave me alone."

"You can't honestly believe that." She dropped the folder onto the coffee table. "Is there anything else I should know?"

If what he'd already said wasn't bad enough, the next part would be like walking across a minefield. "Another engineer who's on the government think-tank has been receiving death threats, too."

Sam sat perfectly still, absorbing what he'd said. "When did they start?"

"Two weeks ago." Telling Sam the engineer and his family had moved to a secret location would only worry her.

"You need more protection than I can give you. If John knew what was happening, he would have sent you to a safe house."

"I'm not leaving."

Sam's eyes narrowed. "In case you missed their message, the terrorist group want you dead. My brief is to help you with your program, not act as your bodyguard."

"I don't need a bodyguard. So far, all they've done is threaten me. They don't know where I am."

"How do you know that?"

"Because they only contact me by email. There's no way they can trace where their messages are going."

Sam frowned. "I'm sure that comforted the engineer who's received death threats."

"The only people who know I'm living here are the chairperson of our project, you, John, and a couple of friends. It's not the first time this has happened and I doubt it will be the last."

"What are you talking about?"

Caleb took a deep breath. "I've worked with the Department of Defense before. Two years ago, I was contracted to help build a program that identifies all terrorist activity across social media sites. Other programs were being used, but none of them were as fast, accurate, or powerful as the one our team created. Thanks to the information we gathered, Homeland Security was able to arrest a cell of terrorists before they blew up three aircraft."

"Did the terrorists belong to the same group who are threatening you now?"

He nodded. "Last week I contacted Richard Lee, the chairperson of the EMP project. That's when he told me another engineer has received death threats."

"Do the terrorists know there's a bug in the program?"

"I don't think so."

Sam stood. "I need to call John."

That was the last thing Caleb wanted. "He won't be able to do anything."

"You'd be surprised."

"I'm not leaving here, Sam."

She turned and looked at him. Her eyes were as cold as arctic ice and just as unforgiving. "This is bigger than either of us. If your program gets into the wrong hands, anything could happen. I'm calling John."

Caleb stared at the whiteboard. Regardless of what Sam's boss said, he wasn't leaving his home. If the Al-Nusra terrorists wanted him dead, they'd have to come and get him.

SAM PACED BACKWARD AND FORWARD. How could she have been so stupid? She thought Caleb lived here because he enjoyed the peace and quiet. Oh, no. He was here because a brutal terrorist group wanted the program he was developing. And if they killed him in the process, it wouldn't matter.

She thought her time in the Army had hardened her reaction to terrorist threats, but she was wrong. For the first time since she'd left the military, she was angry. Worse than angry. Caleb was part of a project that could change the face of modern warfare. He should be doing everything he could to protect himself and his country. But instead of accepting John's help, he was determined to stay in the middle of nowhere, waiting for disaster to strike.

"Is it safe to come inside?" Caleb stood in the living room doorway with a pile of wood in his arms.

"I'm not going to shoot you if that's what you're worried about."

The frown on Caleb's face deepened. "You have a gun?"

Sam nodded. "I work for a high-profile security company. No one goes on an assignment without one."

He stacked the wood beside the fireplace. "I know you're upset, but I'm safe here."

"No one is ever safe. If someone wants to find you, they will."

"They haven't so far."

Sam crossed her arms in front of her chest. "What will happen when they do? The nearest police station is in Polson and that's an hour away. Sapphire Bay doesn't even have an emergency medical clinic. And then there's your home. It's beautiful, but it's not Fort Knox."

"I have security cameras on the main gate and around the house and barn. If anyone steps onto my property, I'll see them before they know I'm here."

"The security cameras won't stop a bullet."

Caleb unzipped his jacket. "Debugging the program is my top priority. I can't afford to be sidetracked by something that might never happen."

"Burying your head in the sand won't make the terrorists go away."

"I know that." Caleb ran his hand through his hair. He seemed as frustrated as Sam. "How about we call it a night and start work first thing in the morning? If we can fix the program, my other problems might disappear."

Sam sighed. The likelihood of that happening was almost zilch, but Caleb wasn't ready to listen to anything she had to say. Perhaps he was right. They were both tired. She couldn't make him accept Fletcher Security's offer of help, even if staying here was the worst decision he could make.

Instead of banging her head against a brick wall, she'd go upstairs and make a list of the things he needed to buy. If he wouldn't leave, she'd make sure he had the best possible chance of surviving when the terrorist group arrived. Because no matter what Caleb said, they would be coming.

THE NEXT MORNING, Caleb looked up from the kitchen table. Sam stopped beside the counter, dressed and ready for the day ahead.

"Hi." Her voice was a husky whisper.

He guessed she was as uncertain as he was about what they would say to each other. "Good morning. You're awake early."

"We don't have much time to fix the program. The sooner we start work, the sooner we'll finish." She took a bowl out of the cupboard and made her usual breakfast of granola, fresh fruit, and yogurt.

"I'm sorry about last night."

Sam's hand paused above the cutlery drawer. "Does that mean you've changed your mind?"

Caleb shook his head. "No, but you said a lot of things that made sense."

"But not enough to convince you to work from another location?"

"You said it yourself—if someone wants to find me, they will. It won't make any difference where I'm living."

Sam opened her mouth to say something, then stopped. "I can't make you leave your home if you don't want to." She handed him a folded sheet of paper. "But I can help you to be better prepared. This is a list of the things I think you should buy or borrow. If you can't get some of the items in Sapphire Bay, we can order them online."

Caleb read the first few lines and frowned. "Survival blankets, trauma kits, and guns I can understand. But cross-country skis and another four-wheeler? Isn't that a bit extreme?"

"Nothing is extreme when you're living in the middle of nowhere. If you can't use your truck, you'll need a different form of transport. While it isn't snowing, four-wheelers will be the fastest way of traveling through the forest. Once winter hits, you can use the snowmobile in the garage."

Caleb rubbed his forehead. "My friend Gabe has a couple of four-wheelers. I'll ask if I can borrow one." He studied the rest of the items on the list. "It looks as though you're preparing for the end of the world."

"I'm giving you the best chance of staying alive." Sam sat at the table and dipped her spoon into her bowl. "Can I ask you a question?"

After reading the list, Caleb had no idea what she'd say. "Sure."

"Why don't you want to leave your house?"

He wrapped his hands around his coffee cup. "When I was younger, Mom and I moved around a lot. Having my own home, somewhere I can relax and be myself, is important to me."

"And you can't feel the same way in another house?"

Only a handful of people knew about his childhood, and they were all part of his mom's family. He didn't talk about the worst years of his life, not even to his closest friends.

It would be easy to tell Sam the same story he'd told other people, but that felt wrong. She'd come here to help him with his computer program and, instead, she was being caught up in something far more dangerous.

So, he took a deep breath and ignored his pounding heart. "My parents divorced when I was four years old. By the time I was thirteen, Mom and I had moved six times. Dad was a violent alcoholic. It didn't matter where we went or how many protection orders we had, he found us." Even now, Caleb could hear his dad yelling at his mom, her screams as his father used her as a punching bag. His mom had done her best to protect Caleb, but nothing she'd said or done had stopped the violence.

"When I was fifteen, Dad found us at my cousin's house. When he hit Mom, my Aunt called the police. He went to prison and, while he was there, we were almost happy. But as soon as he was released, he found us."

Sweat beaded on his forehead. "Mom was in the hospital for more than a month after he attacked her. I never saw my father again."

Sam touched his arm. "I'm sorry."

"My home is more than the walls around me. I spent my childhood terrified of being found. I'm tired of running." Caleb searched her face, hoping she understood how difficult it was to tell her about his life. "This is where I feel safe."

Tears filled her eyes. "I'll do everything I can to keep you safe but, at some stage, we might need help."

"You don't need to stay. I've been living here for eighteen

months and the Al-Nusra haven't found me." The last thing he wanted was to put Sam's life in danger. "You have a family, people who love you."

"And you don't?"

A knot of longing rose in his throat. "Mom died two years ago. I haven't kept in contact with her family."

"You don't need to be related to someone to love them." She squeezed his fingers. "The smallest thing can make you appreciate someone. Take your beef casserole, for example. Did I tell you that it makes my heart flutter?"

Caleb wiped his eyes and smiled. "I thought food was supposed to be the way to a man's heart."

"I've always been a rule breaker." Sam held out her hand. "Come on. We've got a program to fix and a shopping list to fill."

He held her hand and stood beside her. "Thank you."

She looked into his eyes and smiled. "You're welcome."

Sam was so close that her softly spoken words whispered against his skin. Did she feel the change in the air? Did she know how close he was to doing something he would regret?

The smile on her face disappeared. She cleared her throat and stepped away. "I need to…" she looked at the table and picked up her bowl, "…eat my breakfast. I'll be in the office."

And before he could say anything, she left the kitchen.

Caleb sank into his chair. If he thought involving Sam in his messy life was bad, falling in love with her was worse.

CHAPTER 6

For the last couple of days, Sam had kept herself busy. When she needed a break from studying Caleb's program, she'd checked his house, making sure it was secure.

His high-tech security system was impressive. As well as external cameras, infrared beams protected the doorways and windows. An app linked the security system to his satellite phones, letting him know instantly if someone was on the property.

While she was looking around, she'd found two backpacks. After hunting through the house and the garage, they now had half-decent getaway bags, filled with emergency rations and safety equipment.

Then there were the maps. If something happened to the satellite phones, Caleb would have to navigate the old-fashioned way. She'd printed copies off the Internet and sealed them in watertight bags. The sheer size of the property made it impossible to prepare for everything, but she was doing her best to minimize any issues Caleb could face.

On her way back to the office, she looked at the list of

security improvements. Most of her suggestions were easy to implement. Adding extra locks and moving furniture would be quick and inexpensive to change. The other items would give Caleb more options if anything happened.

Caleb walked into the hallway. "Gabe's nearly here with the four-wheeler. Do you want to meet him?"

"Sure. How was the last test?"

"The computer is still crunching the results, but it looks promising." He zipped up his jacket and pulled on a navy blue ski cap.

She stood where she was, wondering why Caleb was still single. He was good looking, had an incredible house, and a job most people would envy. But most of all he was kind, had a great sense of humor, and liked listening to jazz. What more could a woman want?

"Is everything all right?"

"Of course it is." She plastered a polite smile on her face. She'd never felt this drawn to anyone and it worried her. Caleb was a client, and she wouldn't let herself forget it.

She grabbed her jacket and opened the front door. "It's cold out here." She shivered as the sting of the freezing wind tore through her jeans and sweatshirt. By the time she'd pulled on her jacket, her fingers were numb. Connecting the zipper was a nightmare.

"Let me help." Caleb stood in front of her, blocking the worst of the wind.

"I'll be okay." She blew on her hands, then yanked the zipper up to her chin. "See. All done."

He pulled a wooly cap out of his pocket. "You forgot something." He jammed the hat on her head and smiled. "Now you're ready."

A blush worked its way over her face. For a man with such a sad past, he was the sweetest person she knew. In all her time here, he'd never once raised his voice or said a bad word about anyone. She wasn't sure she could have been so forgiving.

A black truck and trailer rolled to a stop beside the garage. As soon as she saw Gabe, she knew why he was Caleb's friend. They were about the same age. He was handsome, in a big city kind of way, and he walked with the confidence of a man who knew what he wanted out of life.

When he reached the veranda, he held out his hand. "You must be Sam. It's good to finally meet you."

"It's nice to meet you, too. Thanks for coming all this way."

"It's no problem. I'm used to oddball requests from Caleb."

"Hey," Caleb groaned. "You're supposed to be my friend."

Gabe smiled. "Friends can still have weird requests. It's just as well you asked me to stop at the general store. Your parcels took up most of their storeroom."

Sam hadn't expected their online purchases to arrive so quickly. "That was fast."

"I must be closer to civilization than you think," Caleb said with a grin.

Gabe turned toward his truck. "We'd better unload everything before we freeze to death. If you move the boxes, I'll drive the four-wheeler off the trailer."

"I'll open the garage door," Sam said, "then help with the parcels."

In next to no time, the trailer was empty, and the boxes of additional equipment were safely stored away.

Sam was stacking the buckets of freeze-dried food when Caleb walked into the garage.

"Where would you like the trauma kits?"

"Leave one with me. Could you take the other one into the kitchen?"

"Sure. I'll make coffee for everyone at the same time."

"That would be great." After Caleb left, Sam studied the boxes pushed against the wall. Between the sleeping bag, tent, water, and food, Caleb would be able to survive for at least eight weeks. And if he agreed to something else she was working on, he'd be safer for a lot longer.

Gabe added another small parcel to their supplies. "Why do I feel like Father Christmas?"

Sam smiled. "It was probably delivering all the boxes. Thank you for bringing them out here."

"You're welcome. Caleb said you're helping with one of his programs."

She didn't know how much Gabe knew about the EMP project, but she wasn't saying anything. "That's right. How long have you known each other?"

"About two years." Gabe's smile turned into a frown as he looked around the garage. "Are you going camping?"

Sam took off her jacket. Gabe didn't realize how close he was to the truth. "I work for a security company. Caleb lives so far from anyone that I suggested he invest in some emergency supplies."

"Including trauma kits?"

She shrugged. "It's good to be prepared. Caleb said you're a writer. It must be an interesting job."

Gabe's gaze sharpened. "It is, although it's a lot different than what most people imagine."

Sam's cell phone rang. It had been so long since anyone had been able to call her that she jumped.

"I'll let you get that."

"Caleb's in the kitchen making coffee," Sam said quickly as she read the caller's name. "I'll be there as soon as I can."

Gabe smiled. "I'll see you there."

Before the phone went to voice mail, she answered the call. Her boss hardly ever contacted her when she was on an assignment. Something must be wrong.

"John?"

"Hi, Sam. How's the program?"

"It's still a work in progress. But we're closer to fixing it than two weeks ago. I'm sending you a report tonight."

"Thanks. I hope you get it working."

So did she. Some days it felt as though they were taking two steps forward and three steps backward. "Is everything all right with my team?"

"They're fine. I spoke with them yesterday and they're happy with how everything's going. Has Caleb changed his mind about moving to a safe house?"

"No. He's still determined to stay here."

"He might want to reconsider his decision. I spoke to some friends in Washington, D.C. The Al-Nusra Nuclei are becoming more active."

Sam's heart sank. "How bad is it?"

"On a scale of one to ten, I'd place the risk of a major incident at an eight. When the terrorist group realizes Caleb is creating the EMP program, they'll stop at nothing to find him."

She took a deep breath. Someone would happily pay millions of dollars for the software. Especially when they were so close to fixing it. "I'll talk to him again."

"If he wants to move to a safe house that's not in Montana, let me know. In the meantime, we've left the keys to option B in the lockbox." John paused. "There's something else you need to know. Caleb's boss has alerted the FBI to what's happening. They have copies of each of the emails Caleb was sent. A special agent will contact him."

"Do you know who it is?"

"William Parker. He's worked with you a few times."

An image of the serious FBI special agent appeared in her head. She was sure he'd do a good job, but he wasn't the most enthusiastic person she'd met.

"I'll let Caleb know." Sam looked at their emergency supplies. They needed to make some important decisions. Regardless of where Caleb wanted to live, she would do her best to make sure he didn't get hurt. But she couldn't perform miracles—and that's what he'd need if he stayed here.

~

"What's going on?" Gabe asked.

Caleb picked up the coffeepot. "What do you mean?"

"It looks as though you're preparing for World War III."

"Ah. You mean the emergency supplies."

"They aren't normal emergency supplies."

Caleb handed his friend a cup of coffee. "Sam wants to make sure I'll be okay."

Gabe left his cup on the kitchen counter. "It's me you're talking to. Are you in trouble?"

"Not yet."

"What does that mean?"

"It means I might have something that someone else wants. If they find me, I'll need more than my truck to get out of here."

"Why didn't you tell me sooner?"

Caleb leaned against the cupboards. "I didn't think it would come to this. If the program I'm working on gets into the wrong hands, there could be serious consequences. I can't afford for that to happen."

"Is that the reason you came here?"

"No, but it's one of the reasons you haven't seen a lot of me."

Gabe crossed his arms in front of his chest. "Are you able to tell me anything about the people who are looking for your program?"

"I can't. The more you know, the more danger you and Natalie could be in."

Gabe sighed. "Just tell me one thing. Are you safe here?"

Caleb didn't want to tell Gabe how *unsafe* he was. That would lead to a discussion that he wasn't ready to have. "I know you're worried about me, but I'm okay. If anything changes, I'll let you know."

A door closed in the hallway and Sam walked into the kitchen. She paused in the doorway and looked at each of them. "Am I interrupting your conversation?"

"Gabe was asking about the emergency supplies."

Sam didn't seem surprised. She looked at Gabe, then back at Caleb. "What did you say?"

"Not enough," Gabe said. "If you need another pair of hands to look after Caleb, I used to be a detective in the NYPD."

Sam smiled. "That would account for the subtle interrogation. You sounded like someone I used to work with in the Army."

Caleb's eyebrows rose. He looked at Gabe, waiting for his explanation.

"I wanted to make sure Sam wasn't a mass murderer." Gabe sent Sam a half apologetic smile. "There aren't a lot of IT specialists who know about trauma kits and what type of ammunition you need for a semiautomatic handgun."

Caleb's head snapped to Sam. "What's Gabe talking about?"

"I bought you a present."

Gabe sipped his coffee. "Good luck with that. I've told Caleb he needs more than one gun, but won't listen to me."

Caleb was beginning to think that having his best friend and Sam in the same room wasn't a good idea. "I don't need another gun."

Sam frowned. "Yes, you do. You have a large property.

Unless you carry your gun with you, it might be too far away when you need it."

Gabe rinsed his cup under the faucet. "On that cheerful note, I'll go home. If you need somewhere to stay, come to my place. I have plenty of room and a few extra guns that Sam might appreciate."

Before Sam got too carried away by the thought of more guns, Caleb followed Gabe out of the house.

One day, this would all be over. He could go back to a normal life. Plan for his future. But right at the moment, the only things that made sense were Sam and Gabe. They were his anchor, the reason he would get through the next few weeks.

Caleb stopped beside Gabe's truck. "Thanks for not making a big deal out of what I told you."

"You know I've always got your back. If you need someone to talk to or somewhere to go, come and see me."

Caleb nodded. "I will. Thanks."

"You forgot to tell me that Sam's not only intelligent and resourceful but beautiful."

"She's a lot more than that."

Gabe studied his face. "You like her."

He nodded. "But I don't know what to do about it."

"For now, you could tell her you appreciate the gun she bought. Sam strikes me as the type of person who likes action over words, but I could be wrong."

"What kind of message does that tell her?"

Gabe opened the driver's door. "That you need her help and you're willing to meet her halfway. Who knows—an extra gun might even save your life. I'll give you a call in a few days."

Caleb said goodbye, then stayed outside until Gabe's truck disappeared from the driveway. He needed to talk to Sam, and find somewhere to store another gun.

~

CALEB FOUND Sam in the office, working on the program. "Can I interrupt you for a few minutes?"

Sam took off her glasses. "Sure. There's something I need to tell you, too."

He pulled a chair across to her desk. "Why did you say I need another gun?"

"While you were in the kitchen, my boss called. He was speaking to some friends in Washington, D.C. The Al-Nusra are causing some issues and they could be looking for you."

That wasn't news to Caleb. "They have been for a while."

Sam shook her head. "I don't think you understand. John sent me some background information on the Al-Nusra Nuclei. They use technology in ways that most terrorist cells don't. Not only do they have access to state-of-the-art computer systems, but they also have access to a range of weapons. Last week they claimed responsibility for a series of bombings in the Middle East."

"I didn't know that."

"John made some inquiries about the engineer on your team who was receiving death threats. He had an accident two days ago and is still in intensive care. It looks as though someone sabotaged his vehicle."

"Was it the Al-Nusra?"

"They haven't said they were responsible, but John and the Department of Defense think they were involved. The chairperson of the EMP Project has called the FBI. Someone will contact you soon."

Caleb rubbed his forehead. "This is getting worse."

"While you're working on this project, the Al-Nusra will never leave you alone." Sam sat straighter in the chair. "There's something else you need to think about. I know you don't want to move to a safe house, but it could be your best chance of staying alive. If they find you—"

"I'll be dead." Caleb closed his eyes. He'd met most of the people on the team only a handful of times. But each of them was well respected—hand-picked for the development of a new technology that would protect America against an EMP attack.

"I have a solution that doesn't involve leaving here permanently. At least, not yet."

Caleb's eyes narrowed. "I'm listening."

"Fletcher Security has been searching for a property you can use in an emergency. There's an empty house about fifteen minutes from here. It's perfect."

"I can't stay in an abandoned house. What if the owners come back?"

"The National Park Service owns the property. The Park Ranger used to live there, but when budgets were cut ten years ago, this area lost a lot of staff. With fewer park rangers, the house wasn't needed."

Caleb frowned. "I've been living here for nearly two years. I've never heard about an abandoned ranger's house."

"That's one of the reasons it's the right property. Most people would have forgotten about it. I can take you there now."

He tried to think logically, to block out everything apart from the cold, hard facts. One of the engineers on his team had already been hurt. Caleb knew the Al-Nusra was a dangerous terrorist group. If they found him, he would have nowhere to go. It made sense to visit the house, then reassess what he'd do after that.

"Okay." He sighed. "I'll look at the house. But I'm not promising I'll stay there." Sam's relieved smile did nothing to lower his stress levels. Working on the program was beginning to feel like the biggest mistake he'd ever made.

"That's great." Sam stood and picked up her jacket. "We can take the four-wheelers. Once winter arrives, you'll be able to use the snowmobile. That's if you're not already living there."

"One step at a time," he warned.

"I wouldn't recommend staying there unless it would make a difference."

Caleb knew that, which was why he was willing to go with her.

He followed Sam into the garage and stared at the boxes of survival equipment. He hoped he never had to use any of it. But burying his head in the sand wasn't going to make the terrorists go away.

"Are you sure the house isn't haunted?" Caleb stepped off his four-wheeler. A chill ran along his spine. The two-story cottage looked like something out of a horror movie. All they needed were a few bolts of lightning or a rumble of thunder to add more drama to the scene.

"It's a little run down, that's all."

Caleb had seen properties that needed to be remodeled. This one required major work. The front veranda dipped like a roller coaster, bowed under the weight of more than one storm and many years of neglect. Windows, covered in dirt and grime, stared blankly back at them. He wouldn't be surprised to see the door slowly open, creaking like old bones as it swung on its hinges.

They'd already maneuvered through a rickety old fence, or what was left of it. What the inside of the house was like was anyone's guess. "Be careful when we go inside," he warned. "Grizzly bears and cougars might have taken over the house."

"It's not that bad." Sam pulled off her helmet and let her gaze wander across the property. "The forest is a good distance from the house. At least you don't need to worry about a tree landing in the living room."

"It's the roof I'm more worried about," Caleb muttered. If the porch was ready to collapse, the rest of the house wouldn't be much better.

"It was probably a lovely house when the rangers were here."

Caleb's eyebrows rose. "It wouldn't make the pages of an architectural magazine now."

"We don't need it to." Sam held onto the shoulder straps of her backpack. "I'm going inside."

Caleb trudged after her. "You do know that breaking and entering is a crime, don't you?"

"When did you become a scaredy cat?" Sam strode toward the veranda. If she heard the loud creak as her foot landed on the bottom stair, she didn't say anything.

"I'm an IT specialist, not a burglar." Was it only him, or had the wind suddenly stopped blowing? "Maybe we should look around first. You know, make sure there aren't people with guns or bazookas waiting for us."

"Once the front door is open, we'll have a quick look inside."

He grabbed hold of her arm. "I mean it, Sam. We should be careful." He lowered his voice. "We don't know who or what's inside. There could be other people living here."

"There weren't any yesterday," she whispered back.

"Yesterday? How did you—"

"John sent two of his team to the property. Connor and Jeremy had a look around and left some supplies in the living room." She bent down and opened a small black box. "They even left us a present." She waved a metal key under his nose. "Now you don't need to worry about breaking the law."

"Why didn't you tell me the house is safe?"

"It was safe yesterday. Who knows what could have happened overnight." She unlocked the door and turned the handle. Nothing happened. "Jeremy warned me about this." She lifted her boot and pushed the left-hand side of the door. It still wouldn't budge.

"Would you like me to try?"

"It just needs a little muscle, that's all." After two more attempts, she gave up. "It's all yours."

Caleb leaned his shoulder against the door. "I think it's sticking farther up. Here goes." He leaned back and slammed his shoulder into the door. The wood groaned its disapproval but gave way all the same. "Who said an IT geek can't be a bad boy every now and then?"

Sam held onto his arm. "You're a bad boy with nice manners." She unzipped her jacket and pulled out her gun. "But even bad boys need to be protected. Stay behind me."

He pulled out his Glock.

"You didn't tell me you brought your gun," she whispered.

"I came prepared."

Sam didn't say anything.

They moved around the house, quickly checking each room.

"It's safe," Sam said when they'd finished. "What do you think?"

Caleb put his gun away and tried to look at the positives. "It's close to my house, sheltered, and off the beaten track."

"Staying here would give the police a chance to get to you if something happened."

He looked around the living room. The best thing he could say about the interior was that it was clean and tidy. And yes, he would be safer here than at his house. But for how long, he wasn't sure.

Sam walked toward the boxes stacked in the middle of the room. "Let's see what's in these."

Before Caleb joined her, he tried one of the light switches. To his surprise, it worked.

"Fletcher Security had the power reconnected," Sam said. "As far as the rest of the world is concerned, there's a new ranger in town."

"I always thought a mid-life career change might be interesting."

"At least you wouldn't get death threats." Sam opened the flaps on another box. "So far I've found towels, toiletries, and pots and pans."

Caleb moved two sleeping bags off the pile and opened another box. "There's crockery in this one. I feel like I'm moving into my first apartment."

Sam looked at him but didn't say anything.

He walked around the room, noticing other things that wouldn't have been left behind by the last ranger. "Whose idea was the taser?"

"Mine. At least I'll know I did everything I could to keep you safe, even if you didn't want my help."

"It's not that I don't want your help. I want to stay in my own house, that's all."

Sam crossed her arms in front of her chest. "I don't think you realize what a dangerous position you're in. The last thing anyone wants is for you to be killed. But there's something even more important than that. If the technology you're developing gets into the wrong hands, everyone will be in trouble."

"I know what could happen."

Sam's eyes turned as dark as the stormy clouds outside. "If you did, we wouldn't be having this discussion. When the threat to your life increases, you won't have a choice about where you go. The FBI will take you to a safe house. They won't care if you don't want to leave." She closed the flaps on the boxes and checked her watch. "We should take a look around the outside of the house. I don't want to be driving home in the dark." She zipped up her jacket and turned toward the hallway.

"Sam, wait."

She kept walking.

He followed her outside. She probably thought he was ungrateful, that he didn't realize how much work had gone into finding this house. But he *did* realize and he *was* grateful.

"I'm sorry," he said when he caught up to her. "I know how hard you've been working. I appreciate everything you've done."

Her glance could have cut diamonds. "It doesn't seem like it. I'm not the only person who's gone out of their way to make sure you're okay. John was right. You're paying me to help you fix your program, not keep you safe."

She took a box off the back of her four-wheeler. "It won't take long to unpack what we brought with us. If you want to do something, you could take the trauma kit into the living room."

For the first time in a long while, Caleb was ashamed of how he'd acted. He'd deliberately ignored Sam's advice when her only goal was to keep him safe. He'd not only disappointed her, but he'd let himself down. And he didn't know how to fix it.

AFTER THE VISIT to the ranger's house, Sam was exhausted. If they were in Bozeman, she would have gone to the gym and pounded out her frustrations on the treadmill. But Caleb had beat her to his home gym and there was no way she'd join him.

Later, while she was catching up on some work, Caleb made dinner. The smell of garlic, ground beef, and other herbs and spices had made her tummy rumble.

By the time they sat down to eat, she was looking forward to dinner and, much to her surprise, Caleb was a good cook.

"Do you like the meatballs?" he asked.

Sam swallowed what she was eating. "They taste great. I like the sauce."

"It was my mom's favorite recipe." He looked down at his plate and kept eating.

Another song began playing on the sound system. With next to no conversation at the table, it was the only thing that made tonight's meal bearable. Apart from the meatballs. She wasn't kidding when she'd said they were great.

Caleb left his cutlery on the side of his plate. "We need to talk."

She wasn't sure they had anything to discuss.

"I know I acted like a jerk. Regardless of why I don't want to leave, staying here doesn't help the other people on my team or the success of the project. I'll make you a promise. If there's any sign that the Al-Nusra are close to finding me, I'll move to the ranger's house."

Sam took a deep breath. "Thank you." She poked at her mashed potatoes. "I'm sorry I lost my temper. It was unprofessional."

"I would have been worse if I were in your shoes. I really am sorry."

"Maybe we've got cabin fever. Apart from the night I spent in Bozeman, I've been staying with you for nearly two weeks. It's not easy sharing your home with a stranger."

Caleb shook his head. "It wasn't that. It was me. From now on, I promise to be more open-minded. You're trying to save my life and protect the program."

Sam studied his face. The dark circles under his eyes had

been there for a few days. But it was the deep lines of worry either side of Caleb's mouth that concerned her the most.

"How do you feel?" she asked.

"Feel?"

"As in having a terrorist group sending you death threats, the success of a multimillion-dollar project hanging in the balance, and a bossy IT manager working alongside you."

Caleb smiled. Only it didn't lessen the worry in his eyes or soften the hard planes of his face. Sam was beginning to realize how much he hid behind his easy-going nature.

He pushed his plate away. "When you put it like that, it's been an interesting few weeks."

"You don't feel overwhelmed?"

"Sometimes. That's one of the reasons I like living here. It puts my life into perspective and keeps me out of the spotlight."

"You might not have that luxury for much longer."

"I know. If we can't fix the program, the terrorist group won't be the only people looking for me. I'll have the Secretary of Defense banging on my door."

"We're making progress." Even to Sam, her words sounded hollow.

"I don't know if the program will be ready for the next phase of testing."

"Neither do I, but we can give it our best shot." She thought about her sister's wedding, the promise she'd made to her family. "I know this is bad timing, but I need to leave here by ten o'clock on Friday morning. Shelley and Jarrod are getting married this weekend."

Caleb's sigh mirrored how she was feeling, but for different reasons.

"I know it's not ideal," Sam said. "But you could come with me. I have a small spare bedroom in my house and a study. In between the wedding rehearsal and family meals, I could work on the program with you."

"That wouldn't be fair on anyone. You should enjoy the time with your family."

"No one will mind. Besides, you'll be safer with me than staying here on your own." He still didn't seem convinced that it would work. "You wouldn't need to come to the wedding. In fact, it would be better if you didn't. The last thing you need is your photo appearing on Facebook."

"Is Shelley still stressed?"

Sam nodded. She was really worried about her sister. She'd called her during the week, but nothing she'd said had made a difference. "I've never seen her like this. Hopefully, she'll feel better once the wedding rehearsal is over."

"I hate to tell you this but, if she's feeling stressed now, it will be worse on Saturday."

"Which is why it would be good for you to come with me. You could keep me sane while Shelley worries about everything."

Caleb leaned back in his chair. "How about we see what happens tomorrow? If the program still isn't working, I'll go to Bozeman with you. If it is working, you can enjoy the time with your family and I'll fly to Washington, D.C. and talk to the project's chairperson."

"It's a deal." Sam checked her watch. "I'd better call Shelley. She's having a major meltdown about the seating plan for the reception."

"Good luck."

"Thanks. I'll need it." Especially if her mom wanted Aunt Rosa and Aunt Maria to sit at the front of the room. It would mean moving Jarrod's best friends to another table—and that was something Shelley didn't want to do.

CHAPTER 7

$\mathcal{C}$aleb stared at Sam. By Thursday night, they still hadn't fixed the program. So, on Friday, he'd driven to Bozeman with her. "What are you doing?"

She gave a nervous squawk and clutched the arm of the sofa. "I'm getting used to the shoes I'm wearing for the wedding."

He looked down at her feet and frowned. "They're high heels. What's the problem?"

"Shelley told me to practice walking in them. Sometimes I wear shoes with heels, but I prefer sneakers and boots."

He had to smile. For the whole time Sam had been staying with him, she'd alternated her shoe choice between a black and brown pair of boots—the heavy-duty kind that withstood electrocution, lawn mowers, and steel bars dropping on your feet.

"She probably meant to practice more than the day before the wedding."

Sam let go of the sofa. "I'm a fast learner. If she hadn't chosen six-inch heels, I'd be okay." She clasped her hands in front of her and slowly walked across the room. "See. I can do it."

Caleb grinned and went back to reading his report.

For most of the four-hour drive to Bozeman, they'd bounced ideas off each other, trying to find a weird reason why the code was failing. Those ideas had started a whole new debugging review. Which was why he was sitting in the living room, staring at lines of code and hoping for a miracle.

He glanced back at Sam. She'd rolled the legs of her tracksuit pants up to her knees and had draped a scarf across her shoulders. He had no idea why, but it looked creative. And kind of cute.

A lot like her house. He should have known he was in for a surprise when he saw the color of her front door. It was mint green. Bright mint green. It matched the pots sitting under the veranda and the mailbox at the front gate.

Because Sam rarely wore anything other than black trousers, white shirts, or jeans, he'd expected her home to be just as smart and practical. No frilly feminine touches or bold colors.

What he'd found was a rainbow of colorful cushions on her sofa, walls of abstract art that sucked you into their depths, and a collection of sparkling glass paperweights. If her living room was a surprise, her kitchen was even more confusing. The canary yellow cabinets and white stone counter made him smile as soon as he'd walked into the room.

"Caleb?"

He looked up and frowned. Sam was staring through the window. "What's wrong?"

"My parents are here. How did they know I was home?"

"Maybe they were driving by and thought they'd see if you'd arrived."

"Or Mrs. Zelanski from across the street called them,"

Sam muttered. "Whatever you do, act like my client. Mom has a thing about me not being married."

"A thing?"

Sam wobbled across to the front door. "She's American-Italian."

He didn't know what difference that made, but he was looking forward to finding out.

Before Sam could open the door, a small, dark-haired woman burst into the room. "Why didn't you tell me you were home?"

Sam's mom was like a mini tornado, wrapping her daughter in a hug before the man behind her closed the door.

Caleb stood and held out his hand to Sam's dad. "Hello. I'm Caleb, Sam's client."

The gray-haired man shook his hand. His eyes crinkled at the corners, almost as though he'd heard what his daughter had said. "I'm Ted, and the woman who isn't letting go of Sam is my wife, Elena. Welcome to Bozeman."

"Thanks. It was a last-minute decision to come with Sam. We're still working on a project together."

Elena let go of Sam and shook his hand. "It's nice to meet you, Caleb. Are you coming to Shelley's wedding?"

From behind her mother's back, Sam was shaking her head.

"No. I'm staying here to catch up on some work. Besides, I don't want to upset the plans you've made."

Sam's shoulders hunched forward. Had he said the wrong thing?

"You don't need to worry about that," Elena said, waving off his perfectly good excuse. "Where do you live, Caleb?"

He glanced at Sam. Outright lying didn't sit well with him, but not answering her question would seem rude.

"Would you like a cup of coffee, Mom?"

Saved by the offer of coffee. He'd take it.

Elena looked at Caleb, then at her daughter. "Not at the moment. Have you remembered that the wedding rehearsal starts at six o'clock?"

Sam nodded. "I'll be there."

Her mom's gaze traveled down the length of Sam's body, stopping at her rolled up tracksuit pants. "What are you wearing?"

"Shelley wanted me to practice wearing my shoes. My bridesmaid's dress is at your house, so I'm pretending I'm wearing it."

The blood drained from Elena's face. "The dresses were sent to Shelley's apartment."

Sam's eyes widened. "They're not there. I called Shelley as soon as we arrived and she said you had them."

Elena clutched her chest. "They can't be missing. Shelley's already a nervous wreck. If she finds out we don't have them, she'll be even more of a mess."

Ted wrapped his arm around his wife's waist. "Take a deep breath. We'll call the boutique and see where the dresses were sent."

"I've got their number." Elena's hand trembled as she pulled her cell phone out of her coat pocket. "I called Emily the other day. Here it is." She held the phone to her ear and waited.

Caleb looked at his watch. It was nearly five o'clock. He didn't know what time the store closed, but Sam's mom might be lucky to get a reply.

Ted must have thought the same thing. "Sam, you stay here and keep trying the boutique. I'll take your mom into town. We might be able to make it to the store before it closes."

Elena ended the call. "Use my phone. If you need me, call your dad."

as quickly as they'd arrived, Elena and Ted left the house.

Sam sat on the edge of the sofa, redialing the boutique's number. "I can't believe we've lost the dresses."

"They have to be somewhere. If you don't have any luck with the boutique, try your other sister. She might know where they've gone."

While Sam was on the phone, Caleb made two cups of coffee. Whoever said weddings were the happiest day of someone's life hadn't been married.

TWO HOURS LATER, Sam stood shivering on the steps of The Holy Rosary Church, wishing like crazy she'd worn knee-high socks under her trousers. She pulled her jacket closer, waiting for the rest of her family to leave the church.

"That went okay."

She turned to Bailey, glad to have some time alone with her sister—even if it was freezing. "It was better than I thought. Why is Shelley so stressed?" She'd hardly smiled during the entire rehearsal. Goodness knows what Jarrod thought of his fiancée.

"I don't know why she's so worried. I've tried talking to her, but she still won't tell me what's wrong."

"Do you think it's Jarrod?"

Bailey shook her head. "If Shelley was upset with him, she would have done something about it. At least we didn't have to tell her the bridesmaids' dresses were missing."

"I can't believe you picked them up from the boutique. Why didn't you tell someone?"

"Mom was getting her hair cut and I couldn't reach you on your cell phone. I thought it would save the store from having to deliver them."

It had definitely done that. But even Emily, the owner of the boutique, had panicked when their mom and dad rushed into the store. "At least Shelley doesn't know what happened."

Bailey wrapped her arms around her waist, shivering despite the thick coat she wore. "Do other brides get this stressed?"

"None that I've met. But you know what Shelley's like. Everything has to be perfect."

"She's not usually this bad, though. I hope Mom and Dad leave the church soon. It's freezing."

Sam stomped her feet on the icy steps. "Your lips are turning blue."

Bailey smiled. "So are yours. How about we tell everyone we'll meet them at the restaurant? We could stop at your house for a coffee."

"Or we could have coffee at the restaurant." She knew what Bailey was doing. She wanted to meet Caleb. Their mom had told everyone about the nice man Sam was working with. And that, of course, had led to a lot of questions she didn't want to answer. So she'd done what any self-respecting female would have done. She'd vaguely answered their questions, then changed the subject.

Her strategy didn't last long. Her family had weddings on the brain. It didn't matter how much she emphasized the point that they were *working* together, nothing short of a miracle would stop them from making sure she found her happy-ever-after.

Bailey blew on her hands. "You know what our family's like. They could be here for another hour. I'll tell Mom and Dad we're going to your place."

"Bailey," she hissed. But it was too late. Her youngest sister was running up the concrete steps, intent on finding her parents before Sam could stop her.

She pulled out her phone and called Caleb. Warning him was the least she could do. And if he was as intelligent as she knew he was, he might decide to visit a mall for a few essential supplies.

&

"YOU NEED TO COME WITH US." Bailey's deep brown eyes pleaded with Caleb. "Shelley will be on her best behavior if you're at the restaurant."

He glanced at Sam. So far, apart from being surprised that he'd opened the front door, she hadn't said much. But that hadn't made a difference to Bailey's excitement at meeting him. Her questions, as well-meaning as they were, made him realize just how careful he had to be.

The other thing he'd discovered was just how alike Sam and her sister were—not in looks—they were like chalk and cheese there. But in how they thought. Their quick minds, easy smiles, and dogged determination were almost identical. Which was why it was getting harder to say no to Bailey.

He cleared his throat. "You won't want to hear this, but you'll survive without me."

Bailey sighed. "You don't know how wrong you are. Shelley has been unbearable over the last couple of weeks. I honestly didn't think she'd come to her bachelorette party."

"What's made Shelley turn into a bridezilla?" Sam asked.

"I have no idea. Everything seemed to get worse when the florist couldn't find any peony roses. And don't get me started on the catering company. When they wanted the final numbers and the deposit for the reception, Shelley fell apart. I thought she might have blown her budget, but the price wasn't any different from what was quoted."

Caleb didn't know much about planning a wedding, but

he didn't think a bunch of flowers and the catering bill was enough to cause anyone a lot of stress.

"We need to corner Shelley and not let her go until she tells us what's wrong," Sam said.

"I don't know how easy that will be. Jarrod's family are coming to the restaurant. Getting her away from the table will be difficult." Bailey checked her watch. "We need to leave."

Sam picked up their empty cups. "We can figure out how to get Shelley on her own on the way to the restaurant." She turned to Caleb. "In spite of the questions my sister has asked and Shelley's weird behavior, you're welcome to join us."

Bailey tapped her finger against her chin. "I might have an idea about how we can get Shelley away from the table." She sent Caleb a loaded stare.

His eyes narrowed. "I know what you're doing. You want me to be a decoy."

Bailey grinned. "Mom and Dad like you. Diverting their attention away from Shelley would be easy for someone who's worked in Washington, D.C. Besides, the restaurant is famous for its barbecue spareribs."

"And they make incredible burgers," Sam added. "The Montana Ale Works is practically world famous."

Caleb didn't answer them right away. He wanted Sam to think he was coming under duress, but Bailey had won him over at the mention of ribs. "Okay. I'll come with you. But don't be surprised if Shelley won't tell you what's wrong."

Sam and Bailey's smiles almost made up for the mess he was stepping into. Only this time, he wasn't the person who'd created it.

～

"IT's OVER," Shelley sobbed.

Sam and Bailey looked at each other. They were halfway to the restaurant when their mom called and told them to come home.

As soon as they'd opened the front door, they knew something was wrong. Their mom had been crying and their dad looked shell-shocked. It wasn't until they'd gone upstairs to see Shelley, that they'd realized how bad it was.

"What do you mean?" Bailey asked.

Shelley blew her nose. "The wedding. It's off. I told Jarrod I can't marry him."

Sam stared at her sister. She couldn't believe what she was hearing. Where was the promise of the 'until death us do part' vows? The 'I'll love you until the end of time' sentiments. Shelley had found her happy ever after. Or so everyone thought.

"Why can't you marry him?" Sam asked.

"We became so caught up in planning the wedding that we forgot about us. I wasn't sure I wanted to get married. But I thought it would be okay, that over time everything would make sense. But it doesn't make sense, nothing does."

Bailey handed Shelley another handful of tissues. "You're supposed to get married tomorrow. Why didn't you tell him sooner?"

"Everyone had put so much effort into making the day special. We'd already paid deposits on almost everything and Jarrod was excited."

Sam would bet a million dollars he wasn't excited now.

"At least you called the wedding off now and not tomorrow," Bailey said soothingly.

"No one is going to understand. People have traveled a long way to be here."

All of that was true, Sam thought. And it wasn't just the travel. They'd bought presents, paid for accommodation. Some of their family had decided to extend their stay and see some of Montana while they were here. If Shelley had told someone why she was worried, they could have done something about it sooner.

"He'll never forgive me." Fresh tears filled Shelley's eyes.

Sam hugged her sister. "Bailey is right. If you'd married Jarrod you would have regretted it. You did the right thing."

"It doesn't feel like it."

Bailey brushed a strand of hair off Shelley's face. "It might not now, but in a few months you'll know you made the right decision."

Sam looked around Shelley's old bedroom. The daisy wallpaper and apricot blankets were as much a part of their childhood as the dolls sitting in the small armchair. All of the issues they'd faced were nothing compared to what was happening now.

She gave her sister another hug. "I'm going to check on Caleb. He's waiting downstairs with Mom and Dad."

"I'm sorry, Shelley said. "You came all this way for nothing."

Sam forced a smile. "Look at the bright side. At least I don't have to wear a frilly dress or high heels."

A watery smile replaced Shelley's tears. "You looked amazing in the dress."

Bailey nodded. "You did. We'll have to go somewhere special so you can wear it."

Sam was happy to say that the chance of that happening was slim to zero. She would leave the frills and flounces to her sisters.

Bailey handed Shelley a box of tissues. "Take these. I'll go downstairs with Sam. Mom and Dad might need a hand to contact everyone."

Shelley wiped her face. "I'll come, too."

Sam followed everyone onto the landing. At least Shelley's tears had stopped flowing. That had to be a step in the right direction. All her sister needed to do now was pay for the wedding that wasn't happening.

CALEB DIALED the next number on the guest list. He didn't know if he was making a difference, but calling people who'd come to Bozeman for the wedding was better than doing nothing.

"I made you a cup of hot chocolate," Elena said. "Thank you for helping us."

Ted put down his cell phone and sighed. "My brother will call my nephews and nieces. How are you doing, Caleb?"

The person he was trying to reach hadn't answered their phone, so he ended the call. "I still have two people to contact."

Elena looked over his shoulder. "I'll do those. Francesca and Thomas will be upset. They've come all the way from Naples." She shook her head. "I can't understand why Shelley didn't tell us sooner."

Shelley and Bailey walked into the living room, followed by Sam.

"I'm sorry, Mom and Dad," Shelley said. "I should have said something. I'll apologize to everyone when I see them tomorrow."

Elena wrapped her arm around her daughter. "At least our family and friends were here for a happy occasion. It's better than traveling hundreds of miles for a funeral."

"That's one way of looking at it," Sam said with a smile. "Besides, we're still meeting for lunch. After everyone's enjoyed the yummy food, they'll forget there wasn't a wedding."

Caleb glanced at Sam. She was trying to make her sister

and parents feel better, but he wasn't sure anyone would forget the non-existent wedding.

"Can we help with anything?" Shelley asked.

Ted shook his head. "Apart from two phone calls, there isn't much else we can do. Jarrod has contacted his family."

"How many people will be at lunch?" Sam asked.

Caleb looked at his list. "Nearly everyone I've called will be there." He looked at Sam's dad.

"I'll need to check with Uncle Gary, but most of the people I've spoken to will be there."

Shelley sat on the edge of the sofa. "At least the food won't go to waste."

Sam sat beside her sister. "And your cake and flowers will be appreciated."

Shelley had asked Father Leo if he knew anyone who needed a wedding cake and a bouquet. It turned out the bride and groom of the wedding after hers hadn't been able to afford either. Without hesitating, Shelley had given them hers, making at least two people happy.

Ted squeezed Shelley's shoulder. "We're meeting everyone at the Emerson Center at eleven o'clock tomorrow. Your mom was thinking of taking a Christmas tree to the venue and calling it an early Christmas lunch."

Sam cleared her throat. "That's a good idea."

"It will be fun," Bailey said a little too brightly. "We could have Christmas music playing in the background."

Shelley's skin turned a delicate shade of white.

"Or maybe not," Bailey said quickly.

"It's a good idea," Shelley said. "It's just…" She burst into tears.

Bailey grabbed a box of tissues off the table. "It will be okay."

"No, it won't," Shelley said between sobs. "Everyone will think I'm an idiot."

Caleb's stomach twisted in knots. Hearing a woman cry reminded him of his mom and the years of abuse she'd lived through. He took a deep breath and focused on Sam. She'd wrapped her arm around her sister, trying to console her.

"No one's going to think you're an idiot," Sam said. "They might be a little annoyed—"

Bailey poked Sam's shoulder.

"It's okay," Shelley said. "I deserve it."

Sam looked at her family and sighed. "Caleb and I should get going. We still have a couple of hours of work ahead of us."

Caleb was so grateful, he almost hugged her. But that would only make her mom even more determined to play matchmaker. So instead of reaching out to her, he focused on Sam's parents. "It was nice meeting you. Thanks for the hot chocolate, Elena."

Sam's mom gave him a hug. "You are a good boy. Don't be put off by what's happened. We're usually quite a normal family."

That produced another round of tears from Shelley.

"On that happy note, it's time we left." Sam gave Caleb a nudge toward the door.

He waved to Sam's sisters and walked into the hallway. At least Sam couldn't say her family was boring.

CHAPTER 8

*S*am picked up a folder and settled onto the sofa. Reading the results of one of the debugging programs was insane, especially after the crazy evening they'd had. But she needed to take her mind off Shelley, and studying lines of code would be perfect.

"I thought you were joking about doing some work." Caleb walked into the living room. "The report can wait until tomorrow."

"I don't mind looking at it now. I'm sorry about tonight."

"It's okay. I've lived through my share of family stuff as well." Caleb sat beside her, stretching his long legs in front of him. "Will Shelley be all right?"

"I hope so. I'm more worried about Jarrod. This must have come as a big shock to him."

"How long had they been dating?"

Sam frowned. "It must be close to four years. Shelley met him about the same time I moved to Bozeman."

"That's a long time."

"It is. You'd think Shelley would know whether she wanted to marry him."

Caleb shrugged. "Relationships are tricky at the best of times."

Sam's brow arched. "Are you speaking from personal experience?"

"I have a lifetime's worth of personal experience." Caleb rubbed his eyes. "I fell in love for the wrong reasons. When I figured out what those reasons were, I couldn't get married."

"Was your girlfriend upset?"

"Not as much as I thought. We both had a lot of unresolved issues. Filling those voids with each other would have ended in disaster. What about you?"

Sam shook her head. "I've never been engaged, but I did think I'd found someone special."

"And?"

"It didn't work out. Our careers made it impossible to spend a lot of time together."

"It's hard when that happens. When did you decide to move to Bozeman?"

"After I was discharged from the Army. I'd always planned on coming home. It just happened a little earlier than I expected." Her hands tightened around the report she'd been studying. "I met my boss when I was working in Washington, D.C. John was looking for someone to join the Technical Development Team at Fletcher Security. When I returned to Bozeman, I talked to him about the job and started four weeks later. Six months ago I was promoted and now I manage the team."

"Are you glad you left the Army?"

"I couldn't have stayed," she said softly.

"What happened?"

A tense silence filled the room. The last few months of her military career had been emotionally exhausting. "A lot of civilians died because of false information my team thought was correct. I saw some bad things in Afghanistan, but nothing that came close to what happened in Kandahar. I was proud to serve my country, but not proud of what we did."

"Mistakes must be made all the time."

Tears filled her eyes. "Not like that." She steadied her breathing and focused on the here and now. Fighting the demons from her past was difficult, but not impossible. With the support of her family and friends, she'd managed to get through the worst days. Her future was a work in progress.

When her heart wasn't pounding quite so hard, she looked at Caleb. There was no pity in his eyes, only an understanding of what was happening.

She took a deep breath. "I was diagnosed with Post Traumatic Stress Disorder. I'm much better, but every now and then it sneaks back."

"PTSD is more common than anyone realizes. I've worked with people who are in high-risk situations. Over time, that kind of pressure can cause a lot of damage."

"It's difficult admitting you have an issue, especially in the Army."

"Why did you enlist?"

She wiped her eyes. "My grandfather was in the Army. He never talked about what he did, but I was so proud of him. When I found out how much it cost to go to college, I decided to enlist. The Army paid my tuition and, in return, I worked in the Military Intelligence Unit. It wasn't until I was discharged that I knew I wanted more from life."

"What do you want?"

She glanced at Caleb. To most people, what she wanted wasn't a big deal. But for someone who didn't trust easily and rarely dated, it was like asking for a return ticket to Mars. "I want friends and family who love me. I want to find someone who appreciates me for who I really am. And one day, I'd like a family of my own."

Caleb didn't laugh. He didn't tell her to dream bigger. Instead, he tilted his head to the side and searched her face. "You'd make a great mom."

His softly spoken words made Sam's throat tighten. "Thank you. Sometimes I feel like I'm asking for the impossible."

"Why?"

"I swapped one job with long hours for another. It's not easy meeting people when you don't know where you'll be from one week to the next."

"You've met me," he said with a smile.

"You're my client. It doesn't count."

Caleb held his hand over his heart. "I'm wounded. You know, some people would say I'm an okay kind of guy."

Sam smiled. "You are. You're funny, kind, handsome, and tall."

"Tall?"

"That's a definite advantage. Most of my friends are about my height. They all want boyfriends who are taller than them. Being tall must increase your chances of finding the perfect girlfriend."

"So far, it hasn't worked."

"That could have something to do with living in the middle of nowhere. Unless you want to date a raccoon or a squirrel, you'll have to go somewhere that has a population of more than one person."

"Like Bozeman?"

Heat flooded Sam's cheeks. "That would work." Until she realized what he meant. "But I'm not introducing you to my friends. I'd feel terrible if you broke their hearts."

"It wasn't your friends I was thinking about."

Sam's eyes widened. Thinking about Caleb being anything other than her client was different from doing something about it. Especially if he was willing to move to Bozeman.

"Why are you still single?" she asked.

Caleb started to say something, then stopped. The teasing gleam in his eyes slowly disappeared. "I was going to say that I've been waiting for the right woman, but that's not entirely true. I'm single because I'm scared. I don't want to trust someone with the deepest, darkest part of who I am, then get hurt when she leaves."

The fear of rejection was just as strong in Sam. It didn't matter how confident she thought she was, when it came to letting someone into her life, she was as terrified as Caleb. "If she's the right person, she won't leave."

"What if I've already met her, only I don't know it?"

"A long time ago, I asked Mom the same question. She told me I'd know who he was as soon as I saw him. That's the worst advice she's ever given me."

"Did it work for her?"

Sam nodded. "Mom came to Bozeman for a friend's engagement party and met Dad. Six months later, they were married."

"There you go. It does happen."

"Not often."

Caleb sighed. "What if the man you were destined to be with was right beside you?"

He was teasing her. She should ignore him, especially when they were sitting in front of an open fire, talking about things that had nothing to do with computers. But ignoring Caleb wasn't easy. So she didn't.

She looked over her shoulder, pretending to search for the man of her dreams. "Where?"

Caleb's exaggerated sigh made her smile. "Here." He pointed to his chest, his face alight with mischief. "I could be the man of your dreams."

"Well, you are tall. And you can be charming." She tilted her head to the side. "But it wouldn't work."

"Why?"

"Because I'd have to be the woman of your dreams." She leaned closer and whispered, "I can't even walk in a pair of high heels. What kind of a dream girl is that?"

Caleb's eyes darkened. "Almost perfect."

Sam searched his face, looking beneath his intense gaze to the man he hid from the world. They both had issues, scars that ran deeper than most people knew. He was asking her to take a leap of faith, to believe they could be more than friends. But there was so much they didn't know about each other. So many things that could go horribly wrong.

Caleb wrapped his hand around hers. "What if I keep thinking about a blond-haired, blue-eyed woman who makes me happy? And what if she wanted children and enjoyed living in the middle of nowhere? What would you suggest I do?"

"I'd ask her if you made her happy."

He cupped the side of her face with his hand. "Do I make you happy?"

The longing in his eyes made Sam wish he wasn't her client. "You make me happy, but I—"

He leaned forward and brushed his lips against hers. Every reason why this wasn't a good idea melted under the heat from his mouth. He teased and cajoled, gave her time to back away before she did something she'd regret.

But she didn't back away. She moved closer, deepened the kiss, gave him the answer he'd been searching for.

Without knowing how, she'd fallen in love with Caleb—and it scared her more than the terrorist group who were looking for him.

∽

THE NEXT DAY, Caleb was awake before dawn. He'd spent most of the night tossing and turning, thinking about Sam. Thinking about the kiss that made him want a whole lot of things he'd never had.

But today was another day. He didn't know how Sam would feel or if she'd want to stay here. What if she thought he'd taken advantage of her? Did she feel safe with him or had he ruined any chance of getting to know her? No matter which way he looked at it, he'd made a big mistake.

Instead of going downstairs, he reread the report he'd printed off yesterday. He needed to bury himself in lines of code, focus on something other than the silky softness of Sam's mouth as she'd kissed him within an inch of his sanity.

Argh. Stop thinking about her. He had less than a week to find the issue with his program. Even if his brain cells weren't cooperating, he had to solve the mystery of the failing software. Reaching across the bed, he picked up his laptop. The problem must be in the interface between the different processes. But where?

Two hours later, he gave up searching for the answer. He jumped in the shower, threw on some clothes, and was sitting in the kitchen eating breakfast by eight. Not bad for someone whose eyeballs felt like roadkill.

Sam's shoes echoed on the stairs.

The granola in his mouth turned to sawdust. He didn't know what to say to her, how last night would affect their relationship. Or even if they had a relationship.

He liked her a lot. More than liked her. She was intelligent, talented, and more patient than he'd ever been. And right now—stunningly beautiful.

His mouth dropped open. "You're wearing a dress."

Sam stopped in the doorway. Her eyes widened and a soft blush filled her cheeks. "Bailey bought it for me last year. I

.nought if we're going with a Christmas-themed lunch, I might as well wear it."

She held the full, knee-length skirt away from her legs. Christmas trees surrounded by snow were painted across the bottom of the fabric. Above the trees, the bright blue sky was dotted with clouds.

The cute, rockabilly style made him smile. "You look beautiful."

Sam's gaze collided with his.

He could have kicked himself. Telling her she was beautiful would make her feel uncomfortable, and that's the last thing he wanted.

He cleared his throat and tried again. "I haven't seen you wearing a dress. It suits you."

"I mostly prefer trousers." She quickly moved around the kitchen, then sat at the table, placing a bowl of granola and yogurt in front of her. "When I was little, jeans were more practical. I used to help Dad on the ranch. I'd muck out the barn and help him move the cattle. We spent a lot of time together, fixing the tractors and anything else that didn't work."

Imagining a much younger version of Sam on the ranch made him smile. "Your dad must have enjoyed your company."

"I enjoyed his, too. Shelley always wanted to play with her dolls and Bailey copied Shelley. Later on, I deliberately didn't wear dresses. Mom eventually gave up trying to change my mind."

"And it stuck?"

"Until I joined the Army. Where do you want to start this morning?" Sam dipped her spoon into her granola.

Caleb frowned. "On the interface that links the last two processes together."

She nodded as she ate her breakfast.

"Do you want to talk about last night?"

Her jaw stopped moving. She finished what was in her mouth, then nodded again. "That's probably a good idea. I'm not proud of what happened."

The bubble of hope inside Caleb burst.

"You're my client. I'm supposed to help you fix your program, not…" She cleared her throat. "It will be better for everyone if I stay in Bozeman. I can still help. It will mean a few phone calls and a lot of—"

"No."

Sam's gaze sharpened. "What do you mean, no?"

"We're close to finding the fault. Working together has sped up the process. If you're in Bozeman, it will make it harder to evaluate the reports we're running and make changes to the program."

"We could use video conference calls."

"It wouldn't be the same."

Sam's spoon banged against the side of her bowl. "I'm trying to protect both of us."

Caleb knew what she was doing. "We're adults. We can work together, finish the project, then see what happens after that." When Sam still seemed uncertain, he added, "We could be finished in the next day or two."

Sam looked at her bowl of granola.

He'd love to know what was going through her mind.

"Okay," she said softly. "We'll work together until your deadline or until we find the fault. But no more kissing."

Even though he wanted to fist pump the air, Caleb kept his expression neutral. They were working against the clock, but at least they were doing it together. And after this was over, they'd have all the time in the world to plan the next part of their lives.

~

"You look amazing," Bailey said to her sister.

Sam twirled in front of her. "Someone with great taste chose the dress."

"It was my one and only chance to get you into something apart from trousers. Where's Caleb?"

"He's talking to Phil. He went to college with him."

"Our cousin, Phil?"

"I know. The chance of that happening has to be a million to one."

"A bit like falling in love." Bailey sighed as she scanned the ballroom. "Shelley spent most of last night in tears. Anyone would think Jarrod was the one who called off the wedding."

"Where is she?"

Bailey pointed across the room. "Over there. Beside Mom. I don't know how long she'll last, but at least she came."

Shelley wasn't the only person who wanted to make a quick getaway. Sam had promised Caleb she'd do her best to help fix his program and, even if it killed her, that's what she'd do. "Caleb and I can't stay for long. We have a lot of work to do."

"I don't think anyone will stay for hours. But you never know. When Mom and Dad's family get together, anything could happen."

Sam couldn't remember the last time both sides of their family had spent time together. They lived so far apart that Facebook posts and family Christmas emails were as close as they came to the real thing. She watched the laughter, the hugs, and the smiles as her family reconnected. It was sad that they didn't see each other more often.

Bailey wrapped her arm around Sam's waist. "I know what you're thinking. We need to plan a family reunion or something. Everyone's having such a good time."

"We could do something next summer. It might make it

easier for everyone to come here." A flash of red caught Sam's eyes. "Is that Aunt Rosa?"

Bailey turned to where she was pointing. "Oh, my goodness. What is she doing?"

Aunt Rosa was twisting and turning on the dance floor. Her bright red, sparkly dress, caught the light, glittering like a disco ball in the middle of the room.

Sam grinned. "She's rock 'n' rolling with Santa."

"Where did she learn to dance like that?"

"Don't you remember Mom telling us about the dances in her parents' living room? Half the neighborhood would arrive with a bottle of wine and the latest records."

Santa, also known as Uncle Jackson, was spinning Aunt Rosa in and out of his arms. For two people in their seventies, they were causing quite a stir.

"I hope I'm like them when I get older," Bailey said wistfully.

Their mom snuck up behind Bailey. "You'll have to find a good man. Rosa struck gold with Jackson. Speaking about good men, where's Caleb?"

The grin on Bailey's face didn't make Sam feel better. She'd only been in the ballroom for half an hour and two cousins had already asked about Caleb. It was as if her entire family had men on their brains.

"Caleb's talking to Phil."

"No, I'm not," he said from beside her. "I've come to see if your dress lives up to its expectations." He held out his hand. "Rock 'n' roll?"

Sam bit her bottom lip. "My dress is all show and no substance. I haven't danced in years."

Caleb's fingers wrapped around hers. If that wasn't enough to make her heart flutter, his wide grin was. "All you have to do is look as though you're enjoying yourself. I'll do the rest."

Sam frowned at the beaming smile her mom sent Caleb. "It's a dance, Mom."

"When you're sixteen, it's a dance. When you're thirty-one, it's called romance."

"It's a dance," she repeated stubbornly. It didn't take much to pull Caleb onto the dance floor. "We need to stay away from Mom. She's close to making you marry me."

"I could do worse."

Sam looked over her shoulder. "Ssh," she whispered. "If anyone hears you, our single days will be numbered. Father Leo will be booked, and Dad will frog-march me down the aisle as Aunt Rosa sings Ave Maria."

Caleb laughed.

"It's not funny. You don't know how determined my family can be. Mom has already warned me about Aunt Sophia's daughter. She said if I don't glue you to my side, Rosie will take you home with her."

"Where does Rosie live?"

Sam's eyes widened. "I thought you were picky about who you dated."

"I'm stretching my comfort zone." Caleb held her in his arms.

"It will have to stretch a long way. Rosie lives in Wisconsin." With one of his hands pressed lightly against her spine and the other holding her hand, Sam was having trouble concentrating. And when Caleb's thumb rubbed the ball of her thumb in slow, steady strokes, she almost melted.

"This isn't rock 'n' roll," she mumbled.

"It's close enough. Does anyone look as though they care?"

Sam lifted her head from his shoulder. Other couples were slow dancing, but they looked as though they belonged together. Hiding from her mother on a dance floor wasn't exactly a recipe for lasting love.

Instead of giving in to the gentle pressure on her back, she poked Caleb in the ribs.

"Oww. What did you do that for?"

"You need to remember our deal. Work first."

"Pleasure second?"

The lazy heat in Caleb's eyes was dangerous. Too dangerous to keep dancing with him. She scanned the room, hunting for either of her sisters. "Oh, look. There's Shelley. We'd better see if she's okay."

Caleb sighed. "Does this mean there's no pleasure tonight?"

Sam's face flamed hotter than a Texas chili. It spiked even farther when her gaze landed on Aunt Rosa.

Her mom's eldest sister was standing behind Caleb.

"You're only young once," her aunt said with a twinkle in her eyes. "Take the pleasure."

Sam dropped her head to her chest. Her whole family was crazy. The sooner they left Bozeman, the better it would be for everyone.

CHAPTER 9

*T*wo days later, Caleb handed Sam another report. "We're nearly there."

She opened the folder, half expecting to see a page of error messages. Since they'd returned from Bozeman, Caleb had been on his best behavior. No casual brushes of his hands against hers, no banging into each other in the kitchen and, most importantly, no kissing.

Sam kept telling herself it was for the best. Focusing on the program was more important than thinking about Caleb. She had a job she enjoyed, people who depended on her. Getting involved with a client was about as intelligent as stepping off a hundred-foot cliff.

She studied the report's first page, then turned to the second. Uncurling her legs from beneath her, she stared in amazement at the code. "I can't believe it." The grin on Caleb's face made her breath catch. "We did it?"

"We not only did it, but we've solved issues I didn't know existed." Caleb pulled her upright. "All eight phases of the program worked perfectly. Congratulations, Ms. Jones.

You've helped create one of the most important electronic defense systems of the twenty-first century."

He wrapped her in his arms, hugging her tight. "I couldn't have finished the program without you."

"You would have managed," she mumbled against his neck. The sweet, tangy scent of pine and woodsmoke tickled her nose.

He leaned back and grinned. "But not as quickly. Thank you."

The warmth in his eyes made Sam sigh. She stepped away and tried not to think about how good it felt to be close to him. "I'm glad I could help. What's next?"

"I need to tidy up a few loose ends, make sure my documentation is correct, then send everything to the Pentagon."

"How long will that take?"

"A couple of days." He walked across to his desk. "I'll email Richard and let him know the program's ready. He'll place the next team on standby." He pulled out his chair and began typing.

Sam wasn't sure whether he wanted her to stay for longer. To be honest, there wasn't a lot she could do, and that was probably a good thing. "While you're doing that, I'll start packing."

Caleb raised his head. "Packing?"

"To go home. My team has been working on my projects as well as their own. They'll be happy to see me."

His smile dimmed. "I thought you'd stay for a few more days."

Sam could have drowned in his gaze. Leaving would be difficult, but she had to go. "I can't stay. You still have a lot of work ahead of you. We can talk after your project's completely finished."

"What about the Al-Nusra?"

"Maybe you were right. They haven't contacted you for a while. It could mean that they've given up trying to find you."

A guilty blush spread across Caleb's face.

"Why didn't you tell me?" She couldn't believe he hadn't said anything.

"I had other things on my mind."

Sam strode across to his desk. "Ignoring their threats won't make them go away. What did their last email say?"

"I don't know. I haven't read it."

She searched Caleb's face to see if he was joking. He wasn't. "Now would be a good time to open it."

Caleb frowned but didn't argue. He scrolled through his emails, clicking on the most recent one from the infamous terrorist cell.

As he read the email, his face lost all its color. "They'll kill my sister if I don't give them the program."

"But you don't have a sister."

Caleb turned the computer screen toward her. "I know, but for some reason they think this woman is related to me."

Sam studied the image. The woman was walking down the aisle of a store, pushing a shopping cart full of groceries. She was probably in her mid-thirties, tall, and slim. With brown hair and an oval face, she did look like Caleb, but that could apply to a lot of people.

She picked up the satellite phone. "My team at Fletcher Security might be able to find her."

A hopeful light filled his eyes. "You think she's my sister?"

"I don't know, but either way, her life could be in danger. Does the email tell you who she is or anything about her?"

"No—only that she's my sister."

Without any information, it would almost be impossible to find her. "Forward me the email. I'll see what my team can do."

After he'd sent the email, Caleb printed off a copy. "I don't remember Mom being pregnant."

"Did she mention anything about your dad having an affair?"

"No, but he used to disappear for days at a time. Mom never knew where he'd gone."

Sam took a folder off the bookcase. Inside were copies of the emails Caleb had received from the terrorist group. She placed the latest one on the table, then one by one, took the others out of the folder.

"What are you doing?"

"Looking for patterns. It's time we started thinking strategically."

"You want to find the person who's sending the emails?"

"I want to find the whole cell. The FBI has been searching for them but, so far, they don't have any leads." She picked up the photo of the mystery woman. "This might be our best hope of locating them."

Caleb took a deep breath. "What should we do next?"

"Keep working on the EMP project. While you're doing that, I'll call Fletcher Security. When I'm finished, I'll give you a hand." Sam left the photo on the table and walked into the hallway. She needed some privacy when she spoke to John.

They had to prepare for the worst, and that could be more traumatic than Caleb realized—especially if the woman in the photo was his sister.

IF SAM THOUGHT yesterday was frantic, today was worse. All the reasons why Caleb lived in the middle of nowhere were thrown out the window. By ten o'clock, the first of two huge

SUVs arrived. Special Agent William Parker was here to talk to Caleb about his family.

Jeremy and Connor arrived an hour later. They both worked at Fletcher Security and were two of the best bodyguards John employed.

And if that wasn't enough excitement for one day, winter finally decided to arrive. Overnight, a storm had created havoc on the roads. Snow sat at least two inches thick on the ground and the temperature had dropped to below zero. It was great news for the ski resorts, but not so great if you needed to make a quick getaway.

The back door opened and Connor strode into the kitchen. "It's freezing out there. Is Caleb in his office?"

"He's in the living room with William. Were you able to install the extra security cameras?" Sam handed him a cup of coffee. Almost as soon as they'd arrived, Connor and Jeremy had driven to the ranger's house. They were hoping to link some new security cameras to the system Caleb already had in place.

"The cameras are ready to go. Once I've added them to Caleb's computer, they should start recording."

"Where's Jeremy?"

"At the ranger's house. He'll test the infrared beams while I'm monitoring the system. I'll be in the office if you need me." He held up his cup. "Thanks for the coffee."

No one was taking Caleb's last email lightly. The terrorist cell wanted the program Caleb had developed. They must have realized their threats were getting them nowhere, so they'd switched tactics. But how had they discovered Caleb's sister? Did they know how much he'd always wanted a sibling? And why tell him about her now?

Sam sat at the kitchen table and opened her laptop. Last night, she'd made a list of everything Caleb knew about his parents. She'd sent the information to the FBI and to her team in Bozeman. While they were doing their best to find the missing link to Caleb's sister, she wanted to investigate something else.

She didn't believe in coincidences. Finding Caleb's sister when the program was almost ready for the next phase of testing didn't add up. Unless someone had leaked the status of the project to the terrorist cell.

If that had happened, they were all in trouble.

～

TWO HOURS LATER, Caleb stuck his head around the living room door. "Is the coast clear?"

Sam looked up from her laptop and smiled. "William has gone to see Jeremy at the ranger's house and Connor's looking around the property."

He walked into the room and flopped into one of the overstuffed chairs. "Why do I feel as though I've been run over by a bus?"

"William talked to you for a while."

"Talking isn't the word I would have chosen. I feel as though I've been interrogated."

"He must be happy that he has more information to work with."

Caleb shrugged. "He was hoping for more."

Sam curled her legs beneath her. "Don't take his attitude personally. He can be…intense."

"He said you've worked together before."

"On a couple of cases. He's a good agent. But if you want to show your appreciation for what he's done, don't give him chocolate brownies. I don't think he likes them."

"Why doesn't that surprise me?" The slow smile on Sam's face made Caleb sigh. If he'd thought living with her would be easy, he was wrong. She was everything he'd ever wanted and, at the moment, everything he couldn't have.

"Try not to be too hard on him. Under all the cool, calm efficiency, there's probably a man with a heart of gold."

"For his sake, I hope so. What would you like for dinner?" The last thing Caleb felt like doing was eating, but cooking was different. If he had something on his mind, he'd bake for hours. The simple act of measuring, mixing, and scraping ingredients into a pan gave his brain a chance to relax.

"There are plenty of leftovers in the kitchen," Sam said. "I'm happy to make a sandwich or something else with them."

"It's no problem. Cooking helps me to de-stress." Sitting in front of a computer for hours on end or being harassed by a terrorist group was enough to make anyone crave the simple things in life.

"In that case, I'll have whatever you're making." She closed the lid of her laptop. "Would you like me to help?"

Caleb grinned. "With relieving my stress?"

"With your cooking," she said dryly. "I can toast bread or grill a variety of options including cheese sandwiches and chicken. If you're feeling really adventurous, you could let me scramble some eggs."

"I was thinking of making lasagna."

Sam bit her bottom lip. "If it comes in a box, I'm your woman."

"No box, but you could still be my woman."

Sam threw a cushion at him. "Not funny."

It wasn't supposed to be, and she knew it. "Well, if you won't be my woman, I suppose you could help me in the kitchen. But you have to follow my directions."

"If we're making lasagna from scratch, I'll do whatever you say."

If he'd known it would be that easy, he would have suggested teaching her how to cook two weeks earlier. "You're half Italian. How come you don't know how to make lasagna?"

"I was usually outside with Dad when Mom was cooking. When I was older, the crash course she gave me didn't include lasagna."

Caleb stood and held out his hand. "Well, from one IT geek to another, welcome on board. I'm sure we'll create a modern-day masterpiece."

Sam wrapped her hand around his.

The warmth and softness of her skin made goose bumps skitter along his arm. He hoped she enjoyed the cooking lesson because, after this was over, he planned on spending a whole lot of time with her. And if some of that time was in the kitchen, he'd die a happy man.

The sound of a foghorn filled the room. Someone or something had activated one of the security cameras.

Sam frowned. "It's probably Jeremy."

"I hope so." He rushed across the room and picked up his satellite phone. "It's not Jeremy. I don't recognize the SUVs."

"How many vehicles?"

"Two."

Sam pulled out her phone. "I'll call everyone. We're going to the ranger's house. Find your getaway bag and meet me in the garage."

Caleb was already heading toward his office—not to grab his getaway bag, but to protect the information on his computer. If any of the data got into the wrong hands, a lot of people's lives could be in danger.

He quickly logged in and activated Clean Sweep, the program that would wipe all documents, folders, and emails from his computer. In a few minutes, everything would be gone. And if they were lucky, escaping to the ranger's house would be just as straightforward.

~

CALEB THREW on his backpack and ran into the garage. Sam already had the snowmobile halfway out the door. Grabbing the other side of the handle, he pulled hard, yanking the vehicle outside.

Sam shoved his helmet into his hands. "I called Jeremy. The two SUVs belong to the FBI. Someone from Al-Nusra is on their way here. William and Jeremy are waiting for us at the ranger's house."

"Why don't we stay here with the special agents?"

"It's too dangerous." Sam sat on the snowmobile and started the engine. "Are you ready?"

He nodded and pulled on the helmet. "Let's go." As soon as he was seated, Sam opened the throttle and flew toward the back of the property. When they drove past the first trees, he looked over his shoulder.

The headlights of the two trucks were close to the house. Sam swerved to the left and he tightened his hold on her. He didn't know where she'd learned to drive a snowmobile, but she wasn't wasting any time. Snow rose behind them, spraying like a waterfall through the air. They zigzagged through the trees, keeping as close as possible to the route they'd chosen.

The ranger's house was close. The abandoned home would give them shelter, warmth, and a place to rest until they knew what was happening. He didn't know how long they'd be there, but it was better than navigating the roads at this time of the afternoon.

Sam yelled something over her shoulder, but he couldn't work out what she'd said. His grip tightened around her waist as she veered to the right, steering the snowmobile away from the house.

Where was she going?

They were heading into another clump of trees. He flinched, felt the sting of a branch as it whipped past his shoulder. More branches scraped his helmet.

Pain exploded in his arm. He glanced at his jacket, expecting to see torn fabric.

Blood.

The red stain grew and the pain tripled. Clenching his jaw, he desperately clung to Sam, hoping she turned toward the house soon. Without warning she veered left, pushing the snowmobile hard across the snow-covered ground.

Taking a deep breath, he ignored the sweat stinging his eyes. Every bump jarred his arm, sending a hot spear of pain through his body. He concentrated on Sam and holding onto her.

The ranger's house was close. Caleb sighed with relief, but they weren't there yet. This time, Sam stayed on course. She kept the throttle open, hurtling across the property like a Formula One driver, only slowing when they were hidden behind the house.

As soon as they stopped, she jumped off the seat. "I saw someone in the..." She looked at Caleb's arm, then into his eyes. Without hesitating, she grabbed hold of him and helped him to his feet. "Hold on. I'll get you inside."

The back door banged open. Jeremy rushed down the stairs. "What happened?"

"Caleb's been shot. I'm not sure where the shooter's gone."

As soon as they were inside, Sam led him into the kitchen. "Sit on the floor while I get the trauma kit."

Jeremy lifted Caleb's backpack off his shoulders. "We need to see how much damage the bullet has done."

Caleb leaned forward as Jeremy carefully removed his jacket. He moved his arm and nearly passed out from the pain.

Sam rushed back into the room. "I saw someone in the

trees. I didn't know they had a gun." She glanced at Caleb's arm. "I'll need more than a pressure bandage."

She hunted through the trauma kit, pulling out a large sterile packet. "This should stop the bleeding."

Jeremy pulled out his satellite phone. "I'll call 9-1-1. We need to get Caleb to the hospital."

"Ask them to send the rescue helicopter." Sam ripped off the packet's seal and pulled out a syringe.

Caleb hated needles almost as much as he hated being shot. The syringe in Sam's hand was about the same size and shape of his worst nightmares.

"What is it?" he asked.

She held it against his arm. "It's called an XStat syringe. The small sponges expand inside your arm. Within a few seconds, they'll seal off the wound."

"Have you used one before?"

Sam's worried blue eyes connected with his. "I've seen medics use them. It's either this or risk bleeding to death."

Caleb nodded and looked away.

"This will hurt but, whatever you do, don't move."

He braced himself against the cupboards. If he thought the pain couldn't get worse, he was wrong. Sam plunged the syringe into his arm, forcing the sponges deep into the wound. Pain exploded inside his body. He yelled, cussing worse than he'd ever done in his life.

When it was finally over, sweat ran down his face. He wanted to vomit.

"It's done."

He closed his eyes and took a deep breath.

Sam held onto his wrist, her fingers cold against his skin. "How do you feel?"

"Sore."

She touched the side of his face. "It's going to be all right."

From where Caleb was sitting, it didn't seem like it.

Jeremy moved from the kitchen window. "The helicopter should be here in about ten minutes. William has arrived."

The special agent ran into the kitchen. He took one look at Caleb and frowned. "Where did you last see the shooter?"

Sam took a sling out of the trauma kit. "He was about five hundred yards north of the house."

William pulled out his phone. "My team will be here in about fifteen minutes. I'll go outside and help Connor."

Caleb tried to focus on what was happening, but everything blurred around the edges.

Sam held his hand. "Take these painkillers. They might help." She dropped two pills into his palm. "Do you need water?"

He started to shake his head, but the whole world tilted at a strange angle. "I don't feel too good."

The last thing he saw was Sam's anxious glance at Jeremy.

He was in trouble, and he knew it.

CHAPTER 10

*J*eremy handed Sam a cup of coffee. "It's not Starbucks, but it tastes okay."

She took the coffee and sighed. As soon as the helicopter landed at the hospital, Caleb had been rushed into the ER and then transferred to the operating room.

The doctor talked to Sam after they'd removed the bullet, but that was nearly two hours ago and she still hadn't seen Caleb. "Do you think he's okay?"

Jeremy sat beside her. "If anything had happened they would have told you. Has anyone contacted Caleb's family?"

"Fletcher Security had his aunt's phone number from when we asked about Caleb's sister. His aunt hoped he got better soon."

"That's it?"

Sam nodded. Thinking about Caleb's family made her realize just how alone he was. Sometimes her sisters were annoying and her mom's matchmaking tendencies drove her insane. But everyone looked out for each other. Not having that support must be hard.

"John called while you were in the bathroom. The FBI is

questioning the shooter. It looks as though he was on his own."

"Why would one person go all the way to the ranger's house? It's miles from anywhere."

"Maybe whoever sent him thought retrieving the program would be quicker with one person."

"Or maybe he's lying. You don't go on a mission without backup. It's too dangerous."

Jeremy studied his cup of coffee. "You might if your target doesn't know you're there. The element of surprise can outweigh having extra people with you."

"But it wasn't a surprise. The FBI was on their way to Caleb's house. Why didn't they warn us that something was happening?"

"You'll have to ask William."

Sam studied the grim look on Jeremy's face. "You think they used us as bait, don't you?"

"It had crossed my mind."

Sam rubbed her forehead. "What's really going on?"

"Don't know, but whatever it is can't be good. On a brighter note, we might have found Caleb's sister. The FBI is sending someone to a house in Milwaukee to take a DNA sample from her."

"Did she know about Caleb?"

Jeremy shook his head. "It doesn't sound like it. She lives around the corner from where he grew up."

"How did that happen?"

"I don't know. His aunt and uncle know nothing about another sibling. The only person who would know about her is Caleb's father."

Sam leaned her head against the wall. "Caleb never talks about his dad. He hasn't seen him in a long time."

"Neither has anyone else. His death hasn't been registered anywhere, so we're assuming he's still alive."

"I'm amazed Caleb was able to make a better life for himself. It couldn't have been easy growing up with a violent father."

Jeremy watched the nurses hurrying past the family waiting room. "Sometimes life throws you lemons. He must have a strong sense of who he is and what he wants from life."

Sam wasn't sure that Caleb's life was working out the way he wanted. He had a high-pressure job that kept him away from the people he cared about. Maybe after this was over, he could find a new kind of normal out of the life he'd created.

Jeremy nudged her arm. "Is that Caleb's doctor?"

Sam stood when the doctor nodded at her.

"Are you Samantha Jones?"

"I am. This is my friend, Jeremy. How's Caleb?"

The doctor shook their hands. "He's doing as well as can be expected. Thanks to your quick thinking he's still alive."

That didn't fill Sam with hope. There was a big difference between being alive and having no permanent damage from the gunshot wound. "Will his arm be okay?"

"There's a lot of muscle damage, but over time, he should be okay."

She breathed a sigh of relief. "Can we see him?"

"Of course you can. But don't stay too long. It's late and he's tired. If you go to the nurses' station, they'll show you which room he's in." He held out his hand. "I'll be back tomorrow afternoon. If Caleb wants to go home, convince him to stay. Another couple of nights at the hospital will help his recovery."

Sam promised she'd do her best, but knowing Caleb, he'd want to leave—especially when he discovered that Fletcher Security had been hired to protect him.

~

THE CURTAIN around Caleb's bed opened. He looked up, expecting to see a nurse with another tray of drugs.

But it wasn't a nurse. It was someone he hadn't stopped thinking about. *Sam.* He studied her pale face, the uncertainty in her eyes.

"It's okay. I'm still alive."

She didn't smile. "I was worried about you."

A tightness filled his throat. No one had worried about him in so long that he didn't know what to say.

Sam slowly walked toward his bed. "The doctor said you'll make a full recovery."

He took a deep breath. If he didn't say something, she'd think the bullet had affected his brain. "I hope so. I can still wiggle my fingers."

Her gaze swept across his body. Three pillows supported his bandaged arm. He moved his fingers and Sam's eyes filled with tears.

He wanted to reach out, pull her close, lean on her strength while both of them came to terms with what had happened. But he didn't. Couldn't. "Did Jeremy come with you?"

Sam nodded. "He'll be here soon. He's letting our boss know you're okay."

"I need to call Gabe, too. I don't know whether he's been trying to contact me."

"Would you like me to call him?"

"I'll do it later." Tears filled Caleb's eyes. He wiped his hand across his face, struggling to control the emotions crashing inside him.

Sam moved closer. "Would you like a hug?"

He barely managed a nod before she wrapped her arms

around him. He buried his face in her neck, holding her tight as the stress and worry of what had happened hit him.

"Everything will be all right," she whispered.

He took a deep breath and focused on the warmth of her hands as she gently rubbed his back, the shape of her body as he relaxed against her. "I don't know what's wrong with me."

She kissed the side of his face. "There's nothing wrong with you. You're in shock and you've just had surgery. It's going to be all right."

Caleb had always prided himself on being level-headed—the person who never panicked or became emotional. But after he was shot, something inside of him snapped.

"What are you thinking about?" Sam's softly spoken words brought more tears to his eyes.

"When I woke up in the helicopter, I realized that everything I thought was important meant nothing. I've worked long hours, spent more time networking than making friends. I deliberately push people away so I don't have to choose between work and them. If I died, it would be like I'd never existed."

Sam rubbed his uninjured arm. "Plenty of people would miss you, including me. But you aren't going to die."

He took a deep, shuddering breath. "I don't want the rest of my life to be a repeat of what I've already done. I want more, Sam."

She touched the side of his face. "That's the amazing thing about your life. You *can* have more. All you need to do is work out what you want."

"What if I don't know what I want?"

"Then you rely on what feels right."

He held her hand. "This feels right."

She squeezed his fingers and sighed. "One day it will feel even better. But not yet. I care about you, Caleb. But I'm here to protect you. If I let my emotions—"

He pulled her close, kissing her with a hunger that left him breathless. Sam's mouth opened and she moved closer, teasing him with the taste and feel of her body, the promise of everything to come. He wanted this, needed to be close to the only woman who'd ever seen the real him. She was his anchor in a stormy sea, the reason he wanted to live.

He lifted his arms to pull her closer and groaned.

Sam jumped off the bed. "Are you all right?"

"I'm fine. I moved my arm, that's all.

"You could have torn the stitches." She looked at the bandage, then into his eyes. "I'm sorry."

The regret in her eyes made him feel terrible. "It's not your fault. I'm the one who kissed you."

She bit her bottom lip. "It was a good kiss."

His shoulders relaxed. They were okay. Sam wouldn't walk out, blame him for stepping over the line she'd drawn around their relationship. "Only good? What about great, amazing, or even awesome?"

"If that makes you feel better, then okay. Our kiss was awesome."

"You could at least say it like you meant it."

Her smile melted his heart. "It was the most awesome kiss ever. Was that better?"

Caleb reached out and held her hand. "Much better. I know you have to be here, but thank you. It means a lot."

"You're welcome, but you thanked me too soon. The nurse gave me strict instructions to only stay for ten minutes."

"I thought you were a rule breaker."

"I've done enough of that today. You need to rest."

The curtain opened and Jeremy moved closer to the bed. "You look better than when I last saw you."

Caleb lowered his head onto the pillows. "I hope so. Thanks for everything you've done."

"You're welcome, but I only followed Sam's instructions."

Sam smiled. "Don't believe him. Jeremy was amazing."

The warmth in her eyes made Caleb's breath catch. He didn't want her to leave.

She held onto his hand. "It will be okay. Jeremy will stay with you overnight, then I'll take over bodyguard duties in the morning."

He swallowed the lump in his throat and nodded. "What happened after I passed out?"

"Not a lot until the helicopter arrived. While we were loading you into it, William and Jeremy found the shooter. But the FBI thinks more than one person was looking for you. The special agents searched as much of the property as they could before it got too dark. They'll resume their search in the morning."

"Where's the shooter now?"

Jeremy leaned against the metal bar at the end of the bed. "He's in the county jail in Polson. Tomorrow, he'll be transferred to Washington, D.C."

Sam rubbed Caleb's arm. "We really need to leave. You look exhausted."

He swallowed his disappointment. "What time will you be back?"

"I'll be here by eight o'clock tomorrow morning. Connor's found a hotel that isn't too far away. Try and get some sleep."

"I will."

Jeremy moved away from the bed. "I'll be outside your room for the rest of the night. If you need anything, just ask."

Caleb nodded. "Thanks." After they left his room, he thought about what Sam had said, the decisions he had to make. Of all the things he wanted in his life, she was the most important. All he needed to do was wait until the terrorist group was caught. Then he could take a step in the right direction—straight toward her.

~

THE NEXT MORNING, Sam walked toward Caleb's room. Jeremy should have been sitting outside, making sure no one except for the hospital staff came into the room. He wasn't there.

She pulled back the curtain and found an empty bed.

She dropped the backpack she'd brought with her and rushed to the nurses' station. Jeremy would have called if Caleb wanted to discharge himself from the hospital. But with nowhere to go and an arm that was in bad shape, he could easily undo the work the surgeon had done yesterday.

"Are you looking for me?"

Sam turned and took a deep breath. Getting less than three hours sleep hadn't set her up for a good day. Especially when Caleb looked as though butter wouldn't melt in his mouth. It was just as well Jeremy was beside him.

She arched an eyebrow, determined not to let Caleb see how worried she was. "You've had a shower."

"More like a wash, but it felt good. I thought I'd better get cleaned up before the nurses evict me. Besides, I wanted to smell nice for when you arrived."

A blush hit Sam's face. "I bet you say that to all the single women you meet."

Caleb's smile was instant. "Only the special ones."

She ignored the dangerous gleam in his eyes and looked at Jeremy. "Did Caleb behave himself last night?"

"He did, but he thinks he's going home today."

Sam sighed. The chance of that happening was about as likely as a mid-winter heatwave hitting Polson.

Jeremy cleared his throat. "I'll get some breakfast from the cafeteria. Do you want anything?"

Sam shook her head. "I'm okay. I had breakfast before I left the hotel." After Jeremy left the room, she moved closer to Caleb. "Do you need a wheelchair?"

His eyes darkened. "All I need is you."

Sam had spent most of the night thinking about Caleb. It hadn't made any difference to what she had to do. For now, protecting him was her first priority. "That's what everyone says when they're full of painkillers. Come on. I'll help you to your room." She held onto his uninjured arm and waited for him to move.

"I mean it, Sam. I thought about what you said. Spending more time with you is important to me."

Her heart pounded. "I thought about you, too. But I can't be part of your life. Not yet."

The light disappeared from his eyes. "We've fixed the program. There's no reason we can't go out together. Unless you don't want to."

Sam shook her head. "It's not that. Let's go back to your room. There's something I need to tell you."

Caleb's jaw clenched tight. "You don't need to explain anything."

"Yes. I do." She studied the disappointment on his face. "It's not what you think."

He still didn't look as though he believed her, but at least he moved forward. They walked in silence across the ward. She'd thought about what she'd say to him, rehearsed the words he wouldn't want to hear. But nothing would make him feel better about the decision his boss had made.

Caleb sat on his bed, resting his arm on the pile of pillows. "What did you want to tell me?"

"My boss called this morning. He wants me to keep working with you."

"But we've fixed the code."

"That isn't why I'm staying. He wants Connor, Jeremy and me to provide you with personal protection."

Caleb pinched the bridge of his nose. "I don't need bodyguards."

"It's not a request. The Department of Defense has hired Fletcher Security to protect you from the terrorists. They want around-the-clock personal protection and daily updates of what's happening."

"I don't want anyone looking after me. Once the terrorists discover that I don't have the program, they won't keep looking for me."

"That's not what your boss said. I didn't get a choice about whether to accept this job or not, and neither do you." Sam prepared herself for the next lot of news. "That's not the only information I was asked to tell you. We can't go back to your house. It's too dangerous."

"You're coming to Washington, D.C. with me?"

"No. We're not going to Washington, D.C. John wants you to stay in Sapphire Bay." When Caleb started to speak, she held up her hand. "Let me finish. Your boss is sending the EMP program to the team who are managing the next set of tests. If they need help, they'll call you. The FBI wants you to stay in Sapphire Bay, too. If the terrorist cell can be located quickly, you may be able to go to Washington, D.C. right away. But that also depends on what the doctor says. If the shooter doesn't tell the FBI anything, I don't know when you'll be able to go home."

Caleb looked through the window beside his bed. "I want a normal life. For the last eight months, I've had to be careful about who I speak to and what I do. I've had enough."

Sam sighed. "I know it's not easy, but you have to let us protect you."

"What about the woman who's supposed to be my sister? Does the FBI think the terrorists will hurt her?"

"They think she could be in danger. William Parker, the special agent who helped us, is with her. She's having a DNA test tomorrow."

"How long will it take to get the results?"

Sam shrugged. "Even with fast-tracking the sample, it could take at least three weeks."

"Do you know her name or anything about her?"

"I don't know her name, but she lives in Milwaukee."

"Are you sure?"

Sam didn't want him to get his hopes up. She didn't know how the woman had been located so quickly, especially when Caleb had no idea she existed. There were so many things about this assignment that didn't make sense, that Sam was beginning to second-guess everything.

"It could be a coincidence that she lives in the same city where you were born. Once we have the DNA results, everyone will be able to make more informed decisions."

"You don't think she's my sister, do you?"

"I don't know whether she is or not. But at least the FBI is making sure nothing happens to her. How would you feel if she is your sister?"

Caleb's frown deepened. "It would be incredible. But she must be as unsure about everything as I am. Especially if the FBI has been talking to her."

There would be a whole lot more going on than Caleb realized. Dealing with the FBI could be intimidating if you weren't used to the way they worked. "She'll be looked after. But for now, we have to concentrate on you. The doctor wants you to stay in the hospital for a few more days. While you're here, I'll find somewhere in Sapphire Bay for us to live."

"If you have trouble finding somewhere, I might be able

to help. My friend Brooke has just moved above her candy store. She's looking for someone to rent her home."

A weight lifted off Sam's shoulders. "Does this mean you're happy to live in town?"

"There are worse places I could be going. I'll be close to Gabe and Natalie, and I can buy Brooke's fudge every day of the week if I want to." Caleb studied her face. "Do you think we'll ever go on a first date?"

Last night, Sam had asked herself the same question. "Not for a while, but that's probably a good thing. You have a lot happening in your life."

"So have you."

Dealing with a runaway bride wasn't nearly as hard as being wanted by a terrorist cell. Shelley would learn to deal with the decision she'd made and her mom would resign herself to not being a grandma anytime soon.

It wouldn't be so easy for Caleb—especially if the woman from Milwaukee were his sister.

THE FOLLOWING DAY, Sam pulled her jacket closer. She studied the building opposite her, the people going into the store. Sweet Treats was the only confectionery shop in Sapphire Bay. Even at the end of October, it was busy. Some of the store's popularity could be because Halloween was only a few days away. The bright orange flashing pumpkins and rows of cute chocolates were bringing people of all ages inside.

She wished her search for a rental property had been as successful. After spending most of the day at the hospital, she'd driven to Sapphire Bay to look for a house. Two hours after she arrived, she'd called Caleb and asked for Brooke's phone number. Her calls kept going to voice mail, so she'd decided to visit Caleb's friend at work.

She stepped closer to the curb and crossed the road. It would be a miracle if Brooke's house were still available. She'd naively thought the cold weather would deter people from wanting accommodation. What she hadn't counted on were the families who came to Flathead Lake to enjoy the skiing, snowboarding, and snowmobiling. Most of the houses she'd seen were only short-term rentals. Sam didn't know how long they'd need a house. It could be two weeks or two months. It all depended on when the FBI found the terrorist cell.

The doorbell jingled as Sam stepped into the store. The sweet, tempting smell of fudge and chocolate tickled her nose. She could have spent all day here, enjoying the home-made candy that was the talk of the town. But she wasn't here to buy more candy. She was here to find somewhere for Caleb to live.

While she waited for Brooke to serve the other customers, she looked in her favorite cabinet. Bars of Russian fudge sat beside trays of caramel and chocolate fudge. Sam bit her bottom lip, imagining the taste and texture of each flavor.

"Hello again. Would you like to try some samples?" Brooke asked.

With a regretful sigh, Sam shook her head and focused on what she was here to do. "Not today, but I'll definitely be back. Could I speak to you for a couple of minutes?"

Brooke looked around the store. Someone else was helping behind the counter, but it was still busy. "If you can wait five minutes, I'll be able to speak to you. Are you still staying with Caleb?"

Sam nodded. It was easier than telling her the whole truth.

Brooke looked at the customers farther along the counter. "I'll be back soon."

While she was waiting, Sam sat at a table and checked her emails.

"Natalie! It's good to see you."

She looked up as Brooke welcomed someone into the store.

A woman about Sam's age, smiled. "It's good to be here. I had to get away from my studio for a few minutes."

"You've come to the right place. I'll be with you soon."

Unless another woman called Natalie lived in Sapphire Bay, the person standing in line was Caleb's friend's fiancée.

For the first time in a long while, Sam imagined what it must be like to have female friends. When she was in the Army, she'd been surrounded by men. Fletcher Security had a slightly better ratio of male to female staff, but not by much. Apart from her sisters, Sam didn't often spend time with other women.

As the people in front of Natalie were served, Sam had a chance to watch the two women interact. They were good friends, that much was obvious. They joked about Natalie's upcoming wedding and worried about how much work they had to fit in before Christmas.

Unlike Natalie and Brooke, Sam had given up rescheduling her work. She just didn't know where she'd be from one week to the next.

When Brooke mentioned some of the Christmas parties she'd been invited to, Sam sighed. Since she'd moved to Bozeman, she'd been so busy that she hadn't considered her nonexistent social life. It had taken Caleb to make her realize what she was missing. And as much as she didn't want to admit it, her sister's canceled wedding made her even more determined to find her happy-ever-after.

By the time Natalie had ordered a hot chocolate, Sam was

feeling sorry for herself. Sometimes having a great career wasn't enough.

"I'm sorry it took so long to get back to you," Brooke said as she sat beside Sam.

"That's okay. I appreciate you taking the time to talk to me. I tried to call, but you've been busy."

"I turn off my cell phone when I'm serving at the front counter. How can I help?"

Sam chose her words carefully. Brooke was a good friend of Caleb's and unless Gabe had talked to her, she wouldn't know Caleb was in the hospital.

"It's about Caleb. He's moving to Sapphire Bay, but I can't find anything for him to rent. He said your house might be available."

"What happened to his home?"

"Nothing. It's perfectly fine, but he had an accident two days ago. Moving here will make it easier to get to doctor's appointments and meet with his physical therapist."

Brooke's eyes widened. "Is he okay?"

"He's better than he was." Brooke didn't seem like the type of person who would over-react, so Sam told her the truth. "He was shot in the arm. He's okay, but he needs to take things slowly for a while."

"How bad is it?"

"No bones were broken, but there's a lot of muscle damage."

"Did the bullet hit an artery?"

Sam took a closer look at Brooke.

"I was a nurse before I moved to Sapphire Bay."

"The brachial artery was damaged."

Brooke's face lost some of its color. "Was he at his house when it happened?"

Sam nodded. "The rescue helicopter flew him to the

hospital in Polson. He went into the operating room almost as soon as he arrived."

Brooke rubbed her temples. "I can't believe that happened. How did you stop the bleeding?"

"I used to be in the Army. The trauma kit in my truck has a supply of XStat. It gave Caleb enough time to get to the hospital."

"It would have saved his life." Brooke took a deep breath. "To answer your question, no one's renting my house at the moment. Caleb's welcome to live there, but I couldn't accept any money from him. He's my friend."

"That's really nice of you, but he wants to pay rent."

Brooke sighed. "We can talk about that after you've seen the house. I can't leave the store for a couple of hours, but if you want to have a look without me, you can."

"That would be great."

"I'll write down the address and give you the keys. I need to use the back half of the garage for storage, but if Caleb's happy with that, he can move in whenever he likes."

Sam couldn't believe how lucky they were. "Do you have a problem with me and another person being his roommates for a while? We're still working together."

"To be honest, it would be a relief knowing you're there, too. He's so busy. Slowing down won't be easy for him."

"He can't be any busier than you are. Each time I come here, the store is full of people."

Brooke sighed. "Sometimes I feel as though I'm juggling so many things that nothing gets done."

"What kind of things don't you have time to do?"

"Marketing and promotions and online sales. I want to sell candy from my website, but I haven't found anyone who can help me."

"What if I told you I might be able to help?"

"Caleb said you're a computer genius, but I don't have a big budget."

Sam grinned. "Depending on what you want, we could trade fudge for computer advice."

Brooke shook her head. "Your time is more valuable than my fudge. But if you want to help, I could tell you what I need, and you could let me know how much it would cost."

"That sounds like a good idea. Is it okay if we talk about it in a week or two? I need to make sure Caleb is okay before I start a new project."

"That's fine. I'll be back soon with my house keys."

While Brooke was gone, Sam watched the people in the candy store. Caleb wasn't the only person who wanted to change their life. Brooke seemed like a nice person, and if they became friends, it would be even better—even if it only lasted for as long as Sam was in Sapphire Bay.

CHAPTER 11

"Watch the concrete path," Sam warned. "It's slippery."

Caleb was tempted to tell Sam it was his arm that was damaged, not his eyes. But he didn't. Instead, he carefully walked along the snow-covered ground toward Brooke's house.

This was the fourth day that Sam, Jeremy, and Connor had looked after him. Finally, after a marathon discussion with his surgeon, the hospital's physical therapist, and a wound nurse, he was allowed to leave Polson. The catch was that he needed to go back to the hospital in a week to check on his progress.

A week he could handle, especially if it meant being away from the constant noise of the busy ward.

Sam unlocked the front door. "Connor brought a few of your things from your home. We thought it would make you feel more comfortable."

"I'll thank him later. Where is he?"

"In town, picking up some supplies."

Caleb stepped into the living room. He'd been to Brooke's

house a few times, but he was still surprised by what he saw. "I didn't realize Brooke was leaving her furniture here."

"Most of it was stored in her garage. Brooke knew we'd look after it, so she asked if we wanted to use it. I guess she bought new things for her apartment." Sam pointed to the sofa. "Sit there for a minute. You look tired." When he didn't move right away, her eyebrows rose. "I'm only trying to help."

"We'll have to talk about that." Caleb sat on the sofa because he *was* tired. But he didn't need Sam looking after him. "You aren't my nurse. I can look after myself."

The front door banged open.

Jeremy stumbled inside with three suitcases. "Where do you want these?"

Caleb glanced at Sam. If he knew her half as well as he thought he did, she'd already decided where everyone was sleeping.

"You're asking me?" The mischievous gleam in her eyes worried him.

Good Lord. He'd never win an argument with her. "Go ahead. Tell me what you've decided."

"The bedroom on the ground floor is the best one for you. It has its own bathroom and we can get you out of the house quickly."

He looked at Jeremy. "Ground floor it is."

"Don't worry," Jeremy said with a grin. "She babies everyone when they aren't well."

"I do not," Sam said stubbornly. "We need to keep Caleb safe and that's what I'm doing."

Caleb liked the idea of her caring about him, even if he was her client.

While Jeremy delivered Caleb's luggage to his room, Sam pulled out her cell phone. She was probably consulting her list of things to do.

"I spoke to Brooke yesterday," she said. "Do you know she used to be a nurse?"

Caleb nodded. He didn't know where this conversation was heading, but he had a feeling he wouldn't like it.

"She has lots of experience with gunshot patients. She said she could help you with the exercises you were given in the hospital."

"She's busy with her store. I'll be okay."

"Brooke wants to help you get better."

Caleb sighed. "Just like your bossiness is your way of telling me you care?"

"Exactly. In a couple of days, I'll back off. But for now, you should listen to me."

"I can tell you're the eldest child."

Sam sat beside him. "My sisters don't listen to me, so being the eldest child makes no difference. If anything, they're worse than I am."

"Has Shelley been telling you what's wrong with your life again?"

A blush stained Sam's cheeks. "She needs to take her own advice and stop telling me what to do."

"It might be her way of coping with what happened."

Sam sent him a withering look. "Her ex-fiancé is a great person. She ended the relationship and now she wants to fix everyone else's life. I love her, but she's crazy." She looked at her cell phone and sighed. "Telling you about my family issues won't make you any safer. I have something for you, then I'll show you the security system Fletcher Security installed."

"They've been here already?"

"You were in the hospital for four days. A lot can happen in that time. And talking about what's happened..." Sam picked up her backpack and pulled out a silver chain. "This is for you."

He held the necklace in his hand. Why on earth was Sam giving him jewelry? "Is it a get well soon present?"

"It's a GPS tracker. Don't take it off."

He handed it back to Sam. "I'll wear it as long as you clip it around my neck."

Her eyes narrowed. "You're not going to kiss me again, are you?"

"Haven't you noticed that I've been on my best behavior?"

She looked at the necklace, then into his eyes. "I have noticed and thank you." She undid the clasp and knelt on the sofa beside him. "You'll need to lean closer. The technical development team made this for you. We're hoping the terrorist group don't realize what it is."

"In case they kidnap me?"

Sam's fingers brushed against his skin. A spark of electricity zipped down his spine and pooled in places he didn't want to think about. He was doomed.

"Something like that." She rested her hands on his shoulders, surveying his new tracking device. "Not bad for a bunch of James Bond wannabes. We might have stumbled on a new line of personal protection merchandise."

"That makes me feel special," Caleb murmured.

Sam rolled her eyes. "It should make you feel safe." She wiggled out of harm's way and consulted her cell phone.

Caleb would have preferred her to stay close, but fate was being unusually cruel to him. "I'll make everyone coffee."

"I'll do that," Jeremy said from the doorway. "Sam can show you the alarm. If you thought the one at your house was top of the line, you should see this one."

"Why do I get the feeling you're trying out new gadgets on me?"

Sam slid her phone into her pocket. "Maybe because we are." She grinned at his disbelieving stare. "I told you you're special. Come on. Let me introduce you to Xion, the world's first fully integrated artificial intelligence personal protection system."

If Sam was looking for something to take his mind off the hole on his arm, she'd found it. "There are other AI security systems on the market. What makes this one unique?"

Sam sent him a knowing smile. "Not only does facial recognition software identify who should be on the property, but a full body scan assesses any changes to your health. Depending on what parameters you've entered, Xion will send the police, the fire department, or security staff to your home. And if that's not enough to make you drool, it will change the lighting, heating, and entertainment options to suit your biometric readings."

"What entertainment options have you added?"

Sam grinned. "Don't get your hopes up. The only options you'll see are the sound system and television."

"You're no fun."

"That's what all my clients say. Are you ready for the computer to scan your body?"

It was his turn to grin. "Should I be naked?"

Sam's cheeks turned crimson. "You'll short-circuit the system if you do that. Fully clothed is fine."

He kissed Sam's hot cheek. "Maybe next time."

"Or maybe not," she whispered back.

Caleb wasn't a betting man, but he knew when the odds were stacked in his favor. Sam was attracted to him and, at some point, they would definitely be naked.

LATER THAT AFTERNOON, Sam's cell phone rang. She looked at the caller display and frowned. "Hi, John. It's Sam."

"Where's Caleb?"

"He's with Jeremy and me at the house we rented in Sapphire Bay."

"Stay there. I had a call from the FBI. Someone tried to kidnap the woman we think is Caleb's sister."

Sam left the office and ran along the hallway. "Hang on a minute." She rushed into the living room. Caleb wasn't there. "Caleb!"

Jeremy ran out of the dining room. "He's in his bedroom. What's happened?"

"Someone tried to kidnap the woman who could be Caleb's sister. Don't let him leave the house."

A sleep-tousled Caleb appeared in the doorway. "Is she all right?"

"I don't know. I'll ask John." She held her cell phone to her ear. "Did you hear Caleb's question?"

"She's okay. The FBI has moved her to another location. If anyone from the Al-Nusra cell contacts Caleb, let me know straight away."

"I will." Sam silently mouthed, "she's okay," to Caleb.

"We haven't heard from the DNA lab. I'll let you know when we get the results."

"That would be great. I'll send through an update tonight from the FBI."

"I'll look out for it. Take care."

After John ended the call, Sam held her phone against her chest. "We have to be extra careful."

Caleb leaned against the doorframe. "Does that mean no trips to the candy store?"

Sam appreciated his attempt to lighten the mood, but they were in a serious situation. "We can't risk anything happening to you."

"I don't want anything happening to me, either."

Jeremy looked through the window at the quiet street. "I'll let Connor know what's happened."

Caleb winced as he moved his arm. "Is there anything I can do?"

"Go back to bed and get some rest," Sam said gently. "We'll let you know if anything else happens." After Caleb left the room, Sam stood beside Jeremy. "What do you think?"

"From what I've heard about the Al-Nusra organization, they don't attempt to kidnap someone without it being successful. They're putting pressure on Caleb, forcing him into a difficult situation. I can almost guarantee he'll receive another email from them in the next couple of hours."

Sam didn't want to ask the next question, but she had to. "Do you think he'll give them the program?"

"If you push the right buttons, most people will eventually crack. We need to make sure he isn't put in that position."

Sam looked over her shoulder. If Caleb heard what she was about to say, he would leave. "I need to make sure he doesn't see any emails from the Al-Nusra Nuclei."

"I'll get his laptop." Jeremy moved toward the office.

Sam wasn't happy with what she was about to do. But if she didn't get access to his emails, more than his life could be in danger.

≈

"Is anyone home?"

Sam looked up as Brooke knocked on the front door. "I'm coming." She closed the lid of her laptop and walked into the hallway. They'd been living in the rental property for more than a week. During that time, Brooke had seen Caleb twice. She made sure he did his arm exercises correctly and helped with anything else they needed.

"Hi, Brooke. Caleb's in the kitchen. Come on through."

"I haven't met Connor before. He seems like a nice person."

The worst thing about being a bodyguard was not being able to tell people what you did. Brooke thought they were working on an important IT project. Which they were, only it was more complicated than she thought.

"He is a nice guy. I've worked with him for more than two years now." Sam opened the kitchen door and smiled at Caleb. With one chocolate cake already in the oven and another being made, the house smelled like a bakery.

Brooke looked through the glass in the oven door. "You didn't tell me you could bake."

Caleb blushed. "It's one of my hidden talents."

"If you want another job you can help me in my candy store."

"Thanks for the offer, but I'll stick with my day job. Would you like a cup of coffee before we start?"

Brooke shook her head. "Not right now. I had one before I left work. Are you ready for our exercise session?"

"As ready as I'll ever be."

Sam knew how much effort it took for Caleb to move his arm, but he was determined to regain full mobility. "Don't worry," she said. "I'll finish the second cake."

Caleb handed Sam the recipe book. "Follow the instructions."

She sighed. "That's what you always say."

"If you listened, I wouldn't need to repeat myself."

Working for a successful security company meant nothing when you were baking—especially when her best cake effort ended in disaster.

She scowled at Caleb. "You still ate the cake."

"It tasted great, but it looked like a pancake."

"I can't help it if the self-rising and plain flour look the same."

Caleb sent her a sympathetic smile. "I feel your pain, but relying on the color of the wrapper won't help. You need to read the label. Luckily for us, the flour you'll need is already in the bowl. Just add the cocoa, an egg, and milk."

Sam looked in the bowl. If she could fix the code on one of the most complex programs she'd ever seen, she could make a cake rise. "By the time you've finished with Brooke, a fluffy cake will be sitting on the counter."

He tapped the end of her nose. "I'll look forward to it. See you soon."

Brooke smiled at Sam. "Don't worry. The first batch of fudge I made was horrible. All you need to do is keep practicing and eventually you'll create a wonderful cake."

Sam knew she was being kind, but what Brooke didn't know was that she'd been trying to perfect her baking skills for a long time. And they weren't getting any better.

"Enjoy your therapy session." Sam's forced enthusiasm must have been a little too much.

Caleb's eyebrows rose. "If you get stuck, ask Connor."

Her smile disappeared. There were some things her work colleagues didn't need to know, and her baking issues were one of them. Especially when everyone complimented her on the fancy cakes she brought into work—the ones she told them she'd spent hours creating in her kitchen.

WHILE CALEB WENT through his exercises with Brooke, Sam added the ingredients to the mixing bowl. She remembered to fold, not beat the batter, and at the last minute added a few drops of vanilla essence. If this cake didn't work, nothing would.

Hot air blasted out of the oven as she opened the door. In forty minutes, she'd have an amazing chocolate cake to show

Caleb. Her days of pretending to know what she was doing in the kitchen would be over, and Caleb's patience would be rewarded. Or maybe not.

Her cell phone beeped.

She quickly slid the cake tin into the oven and looked at her phone. Someone had sent Caleb an email.

After checking the hallway, she closed the kitchen door and opened her laptop. Unlike most hacking programs, Sam wasn't directly logging into Caleb's email account. She'd created a gateway account on a different server. It collected all of Caleb's incoming emails, only releasing them after she'd checked them. As long as she marked them as unread, Caleb wouldn't know what she was doing.

She bit her bottom lip. The email was from someone called Harry Blake—the same name the Al-Nusra cell used to send their emails. The FBI already knew it was a fake account but, so far, they hadn't managed to find the original sender.

She double-clicked the message, holding her breath as she opened the attachment.

A photo of the woman they claimed was Caleb's sister appeared on the screen. But this time, she had a little blond-haired girl with her. If the image wasn't enough to send chills down Sam's spine, the message was. If Caleb didn't send them the program he'd created, the little girl would be killed.

With a trembling hand, she forwarded the email to her boss and deleted it from Caleb's account. If the terrorist group's intention was to force Caleb into handing over the program, they were doing everything right. She just hoped they never realized their emails were being intercepted. If they did, no one would be safe, including the little girl in the photo.

~

THE NEXT MORNING, Caleb finished reading the report the chairperson of the EMP project had sent through. So far, the program was passing all of its testing parameters. The team had solved three technical issues and streamlined another part of the program. All in all, everyone was happy with their progress—but that didn't stop Caleb from wanting to be in Washington, D.C.

It was nearly two weeks since he'd been shot and he was going stir crazy. He hadn't left the house in five days, eight hours, and forty-one minutes. His life was slipping through his fingers and there wasn't a thing he could do about it.

A light tap on the door pulled his attention away from the sorry state of his life.

"Am I interrupting something?"

He smiled at Gabe, glad of the distraction. Like everything else in Caleb's life, Gabe's visit was preplanned, right down to the time they anticipated him leaving. "Did you get your last chapter written?"

"It took a lot of blood, sweat, and tears, but it's finished."

"Was it your blood, sweat, and tears or your characters'?"

"My characters'. Zac Connelly was playing hardball with a career criminal. It didn't end well."

"Sounds like my life at the moment." Caleb stood and walked into the hallway. "Come into the kitchen. If we're lucky, there might be some cookies left."

"Where's Sam? I thought she was supposed to be here all the time."

When Gabe visited Caleb in the hospital, Caleb had told him everything. Apart from the terrorists' death threats, nothing seemed to have surprised Gabe. Whether that was because his friend had a good imagination or because he was used to writing about murder and mayhem, he didn't know.

Caleb looked in the pantry for the cookies. "Sam's upstairs sleeping. It was her turn to do the night shift."

Gabe sat on a kitchen stool. "So, how's it all going?"

"My arm is slowly healing. It will take longer than I thought to repair the muscle, but I'll get there. We haven't heard from the terrorist group and there's no news about whether I have a sister or not."

"You should write a book about what's happened."

Caleb opened a packet of cookies and left them on the counter. "No one would believe me."

"Most of the stuff in my books is make-believe. Your story is one hundred percent real. You can't get more authentic than that."

"I don't need authentic. I need a happy ending."

Gabe sighed. "You and me both. What's happening with Sam?"

Caleb frowned. "What do you mean?"

"The last time I saw you together there was a definite spark. Do you still like her?"

Caleb poured hot coffee into two cups. "I more than like her, but sparks can be dangerous. Nothing will happen while she's working with me."

"Are you sure about that?"

"Unfortunately, yes." Talking about Sam was the last thing he wanted to do. She'd gotten under his skin, left Caleb so darn confused that he just wanted her bodyguard duties to be over.

"Her assignment with you won't last forever. Once the FBI finds the terrorist cell your life will go back to normal."

Caleb cradled his coffee cup between his hands. "The American cell is part of a larger organization. What if this is bigger than anyone realizes? All it would take is someone to create a program that neutralizes the EMP program and all the work we've done will be for nothing."

"They have to get their hands on the program first."

"There's already been one breach in security. Who's to say the same person won't give the program to the terrorists?"

Gabe studied Caleb's face. "You can't be in control of every aspect of the project. That's why you report to the chairperson."

Caleb took a deep breath. If someone from outside their team got hold of the program, it wouldn't matter who was in charge. The effect would be the same—total and utter chaos if an EMP attack were launched.

The back door opened and Connor came inside. "Sorry to interrupt, but you need to call John right away, Caleb. The DNA results have come back from the lab."

CHAPTER 12

$\mathcal{C}$aleb sat on the kitchen stool, staring through the window.

"Here. Drink this. You look as though you need it." Gabe handed him a fresh cup of coffee and sat beside him. "Is everything all right?"

He shook his head, still in shock. John had told him much more than the results of the DNA test. "I have a sister."

"A half sister or a sister who has the same parents as you?"

"A full sister."

Gabe's eyes widened. "How did that happen?"

"I don't know. Mom never mentioned having other children. And Dad..." His voice trailed off as he thought about the man who was worse than a stranger to him. "He never talked about having a daughter."

Gabe leaned against the kitchen counter. "Did you find any photos or documents after your mom died that didn't make sense?"

"Nothing."

"Do you know your sister's name or anything about her?"

"Her name is Megan Stevenson. She's thirty-four years old and lives in Milwaukee with her five-year-old niece."

Gabe frowned. "What does she know about you?"

Caleb dropped his head to his chest. "About the same as I've been told about her." He took a deep breath, still not believing he had a sister. "I used to dream about having a brother or sister and now that I do, I…" He swallowed the knot in his throat. "I feel so guilty. She didn't ask to be part of what's happening."

"Where is she now?"

"I don't know. The FBI has taken her to a safe house. She must be terrified."

Gabe sighed. "At least she's safe."

Caleb wiped his hands on his jeans. "I'll be back soon. I have to talk to Sam." And with more purpose than he'd felt in a long time, he walked out of the kitchen. There was only one thing on his mind.

This had to end.

～

SAM RUBBED HER EYES. "Slow down. I've just woken up."

"The woman in the photo is my sister. I don't want her to get hurt."

"No one does. That's why William was sent to Milwaukee." She pushed her blankets off her legs and yawned. "If we're going to talk, I need to get out of my pajamas. Shoo."

Caleb looked around her bedroom. He picked up a pair of jeans she'd left over the back of the chair. "Gabe's downstairs. Do you want to wear your jeans?"

She slid open the curtains, blinking against the mid-morning sunlight. "I can dress myself. Go and talk to Gabe. He'll think you've forgotten about him."

Sam didn't wait for Caleb's reply. She picked up the

bundle of clothes she kept beside her bed and walked into the bathroom. Her getaway clothes wouldn't make any fashion statement, but they were clean, tidy, and warm. Everything that was essential when you were on the run from a group of terrorists.

Another yawn locked her jaw in place. When she worked the night shift, she usually slept until two o'clock in the afternoon. This morning, she'd barely rested her head on the pillow when Caleb stormed into her room.

If he hadn't said something as soon as he shook her awake, he would have been flat on his back, nursing more than a hole in his arm.

She threw on her clothes and opened the bathroom door. Caleb was leaning against the wall, waiting for her. "Aren't you supposed to be keeping Gabe company?"

"I wanted to make sure you didn't go back to bed."

"Who me?" She thought about her super comfy inner-sprung mattress. It was so tempting to turn around and snooze the rest of the day away.

Caleb must have sensed her dilemma. He held out his hand, coaxing her into staying with him instead of going back to bed. "I have something important I want to discuss with you."

Sam sighed. How could she resist his earnest blue eyes or the pleading tone in his voice? She placed her hand in his and frowned. He'd had the same expression on his face when he'd told her he wanted to live a normal life. And normal could only mean one thing.

"You're not moving back to your house."

His eyes widened. "How did you know what I was going to say?"

"Call it a sixth sense." She let go of his hand and poked him in the chest. "Under no circumstances are you going back. It's too dangerous."

"The terrorist group are out of control. Someone has to stop them."

"And you think a one-armed IT consultant from Milwaukee will do that?"

Caleb straightened his spine. "It's better than doing nothing. I could draw them into the open and let you take care of everything else."

"The FBI, the Department of Defense, *and* Fletcher Security are looking for the terrorists. Our job is to keep you safe. *Your* job is to do what you're told. If you don't, you could end up with more than a hole in your arm."

"They've already tried to kidnap my sister. If they find her, they might kill her."

Sam knew they could do a whole lot worse than that. His sister's five-year-old niece was in their firing line. If the FBI overlooked anything, their mistake could be deadly. "Your sister has gone into hiding. No one will find her."

"Just like they wouldn't find us? No one should have known about the ranger's house."

Sam rubbed her temples. She'd spent a lot of time thinking about the same thing. Hopefully, in the next few days, they would have more answers. But for now, she had to focus on what was happening in Sapphire Bay. "I'm going to the kitchen. I need a drink." She walked around Caleb and headed toward the stairs.

"You know something isn't right. We have to stop them."

"There isn't anything we can do."

"We could change tactics." Caleb followed her down the stairs. "If we trick them into thinking I'm on my own, they might make a mistake."

"If the man who shot you is like the rest of the group, I wouldn't hold my breath. He still hasn't told anyone about the cell or how he knew we would go to the ranger's house."

Sam walked into the kitchen and waved at Gabe. "Hi. Can

you talk some sense into Caleb? He wants to go back to his house."

"I hope you're joking."

Sam poured herself a coffee. "Unfortunately not."

Gabe's brown eyes focused on Caleb. "I don't care how clever you are with computers. That has to be the dumbest idea you've ever had."

"What else can we do?"

Cold dread crept along Sam's spine. "We stay here and be safe." Someone had to find the terrorist cell, but it wouldn't be Caleb. He had more important things to do, like stay alive.

AT TWO O'CLOCK THE next morning, Sam sat at the kitchen counter, studying a document on her laptop. She hadn't been completely honest with Caleb when she'd told him there was nothing they could do. There was plenty. Only most of it was happening in Washington, D.C.

A week ago, John Fletcher contacted some people he knew at the Department of Defense. What they'd told him hadn't been reassuring. After reviewing everything that had happened, there were too many overlapping events to make the Al-Nusra's actions a set of random coincidences.

What Caleb had said was true. The Al-Nusra terrorists had to be stopped, but it would take more resources than anyone had anticipated.

Sam leaned forward as she read about each person in the EMP project team.

Caleb's boss, Richard Lee, was a respected member of the special operations task force. He was divorced and raising his two daughters on his own. By all accounts, his quick, intelligent mind and quirky sense of humor made him a good project leader. With no criminal convictions or affiliations to other groups of interest, he hadn't raised any red flags.

The man who had been involved in the car accident was still in the hospital, but out of intensive care. Married with three children, Elijah Jackson lived an hour from work. He spent most of his free time restoring old vehicles and was a valued member of the team. She glanced through his work history. There were no international appointments, nothing to suggest he was involved in the Al-Nusra's plans to steal the EMP software.

Sam turned to the next person's profile. Searching for trigger points was like looking through a telescope, hoping to find proof that there was life on Mars. The eighty-page report only scratched the surface of what motivated people. The usual stress indicators were there; divorce, the death of close family members, health scares, and unexpected financial issues. But that didn't mean any of the EMP team would commit cyberterrorism.

None of Caleb's colleagues had criminal convictions, their family lives seemed relatively stable, and no one had a history of unpredictable or erratic behavior.

She turned to another profile and sighed. There were a lot of factors that made someone a likely candidate for blackmail. Looking through the document could be a complete waste of time or she could be missing the obvious.

Sam kept reading for another half hour before pushing her laptop away. What was she missing? Out of every profile she'd read, Caleb's boss made her the most uneasy. Why did Richard Lee raise red flags for her and no one else? Being a single dad didn't make you more likely to help a terrorist organization. But it did make you more vulnerable, especially to groups as unscrupulous as the Al-Nusra.

She checked her watch and walked toward Caleb's new work space. Connor and Jeremy had brought everything from his old office and left them in Brooke's house. At the moment, the photos and documents were spread across a table. Seeing them in a different setting might unravel the confusion in her mind. Or create even more questions.

A wooden stair creaked.

She spun around, yanked her gun out of its holster, and pointed it at the staircase.

Caleb froze. "It's me."

Sam took a deep breath. "You should be asleep," she whispered.

He walked down the last few stairs, totally oblivious to what could have happened. "I couldn't sleep. I thought I'd make myself a hot chocolate. Would you like one?"

She thought about her open laptop, the report she didn't want him to see. "Sure. I'll turn on the kettle."

Moving quickly, she walked into the kitchen, closed the lid of her laptop and filled the kettle with water. "Why can't you sleep?"

"Too much on my mind."

"We're here to help you. Leave the worrying to us."

Caleb took two cups out of the cupboard. "That's easier said than done."

Sam watched him open the canister of cocoa powder. "You aren't worried about your appointment at the hospital, are you?"

He shook his head. "I've been doing the exercises and Brooke's happy with my progress. How's your sister?"

"It depends on which one you mean. Shelley has gone back to work. She's returned all the wedding presents that were mailed to her and paid for the things she couldn't cancel. Bailey is thinking of starting her own family therapy center. She's looking at different properties."

"In Bozeman?"

"No. Most of the buildings are north of Bozeman. Bailey

wasn't like me. She never wanted to leave home. But after Shelley's wedding fiasco, she wants to try something new."

"Have the Facebook posts stopped?"

"They have, thank goodness." Sam had shown Caleb the social media summary of Shelley's canceled wedding. The Bozeman Community Facebook page had been full of speculation. Everyone seemed to have a reason why Shelley didn't get married. Unbelievably, it had taken more than four weeks for people to stop posting comments.

Sam poured hot water into the cups. "If you know anyone who needs a beautiful satin wedding dress, let me know. If Shelley can't find someone who wants it, she'll donate it to The Bridesmaids Club."

"The only person I know who's getting married is Natalie. I'm almost certain she's organized her dress by now, but I'll ask." He tilted his head to the side. "This might be a silly question, but what's The Bridesmaids Club?"

Sam smiled. It was a welcome relief to talk about something that didn't involve guns or terrorists. "A few years ago, a group of friends gave their old bridesmaids' dresses to a bride who'd had hers stolen. A story about what they did appeared in the newspaper and, before they knew it, gowns from around the country were sent to them. The group of friends gave the dresses to women who couldn't afford them. That's why they call themselves, The Bridesmaids Club. Now, they get sent bridal gowns, tiaras, shoes, and even jewelry. They've helped hundreds of people create the wedding of their dreams."

"That sounds like the perfect good news story."

Sam handed Caleb a cup of hot chocolate. "It is. Talking about good news stories, do you know anything about e-commerce programs? I'm helping Brooke update her website. She wants to sell her candy online."

"I have no idea how they work. But if you're happy to

wait until later today, I'll have a look after my hospital appointment."

"That would be great. I promised Brooke I'd have a meeting with her by the end of next week. I'd like to take some options for her to think about." Sam picked up her cup. "I should go back to your office and check the security cameras. If you need anything, just text or call me."

Caleb nodded. "I'll stay here for a few more minutes, then go back to bed. Is there anything you need from Polson?"

"Not at the moment. If I think of anything, I'll let you know." Sam took her laptop off the counter and left the kitchen. At least she'd dodged one disaster. The next one might not be so easy to avoid.

AFTER SAM LEFT THE KITCHEN, Caleb pulled out his satellite phone. What he was about to do went against everything he knew was right. You never gave terrorists what they wanted. While he appreciated the sentiment, it didn't help the people around him. There was a quick way to end what was happening and he wouldn't miss his opportunity.

If the Al-Nusra Nuclei wanted the program, they'd have to meet him in person, not make threats over the Internet. There would be no more car accidents and no more kidnapping attempts.

For his entire childhood, he'd dreamed of having a sibling to share the good and not so good times with. Now that he knew he had a sister, he'd do everything he could to keep her safe.

He opened his email and scrolled through the list of messages. The last email from the terrorist cell had arrived a week ago. He'd expected the barrage of threats to continue, but they hadn't. Their silence was just as worrying as the emails.

He found what he was looking for and pressed the reply button. If he didn't make them come into the open, no one would ever find them. And if someone died, he'd never be able to live with himself.

Looking over his shoulder, he listened for Sam's footsteps on the wooden floor. Apart from the hum of the refrigerator, the house was silent.

After he'd typed a quick message, he dropped his satellite phone onto the counter. The damage had been done. Now all he could do was wait.

CHAPTER 13

*B*y six o'clock in the morning, Sam was exhausted. As well as making sure the house was secure, she'd spent her time going over the information they'd collected about the Al-Nusra Nuclei. She re-checked Caleb's emails, looked for clues in the language they used, the way they structured their sentences. She'd even studied the photos they'd sent, looking for anything that could tell her where they were hiding.

As far as she could tell, at least three people were responsible for the emails Caleb had received. The words were similar, but minute grammatical differences became glaringly obvious when she compared the messages. But that wasn't enough to locate them. The emails could have been sent from someone working in a warehouse in Arlington or from a yacht in the Gulf of Mexico.

She ran her hands through her hair and sighed. No one was any closer to finding the terrorists, and that worried her. The longer they remained unidentified, the more havoc they could cause.

Sam took off her glasses and glanced at the kitchen clock.

She had more than enough time to do a final sweep of the property before Connor arrived for the morning shift.

As she pulled on her jacket, she peered through the kitchen window. The shadowy gray of the pre-dawn sky made everything appear more dangerous than it was. Even so, she checked her holster, making sure her gun was where it had been all night.

When her cell phone beeped, she frowned at the screen. Caleb had received another email.

After five days with no contact from the terrorists, she was hoping they'd realized they wouldn't get what they wanted. But obviously not.

She walked across to her laptop and typed in her password. This message was different.

Bile rose in her throat. A photo of a middle-aged man filled the screen. Dark hair flopped over a face that was a bloody, bruised mess. There were no words, only the haunting image of a man who feared for his life.

He had to be working on the EMP project team with Caleb.

Sam quickly opened the electronic document her boss had sent her. She flicked through the profiles of the people, stopping at one of the photos.

Anthony Sorenson was a retired physics lecturer. A year ago, Anthony and his wife had moved to Spokane to be closer to his daughter and their grandchildren.

She pushed aside the horror of what was happening. Before anyone came downstairs, she forwarded the email to her boss, then sent him an urgent text. John would send it to a team of analysts and to the FBI. She just prayed that someone, somewhere, was watching over Anthony. Because if they couldn't find him, he could be gone forever.

~

CALEB WALKED into the hospital at Polson. He moved quickly across the main reception area, heading toward the elevators. Jeremy walked beside him and Connor followed closely behind. Instead of enjoying his time away from Sapphire Bay, he felt like a criminal being transported between prisons.

Something wasn't right. From the moment he'd seen his bodyguards this morning, they'd been tense, double-checking every aspect of the drive into Polson. They were taking two vehicles—not because they wanted to give Caleb time on his own, but because it would give them options if something happened.

Something *had* happened, but they refused to talk about it. They couldn't know about the email he'd sent to the terrorists. And if it wasn't that, he didn't know what had put them on alert. Maybe he was overreacting. What he planned on doing today was plain crazy, but he couldn't think of another way of stopping this madness.

Jeremy stood behind a group of people waiting for the elevator. His gaze swept across the crowd, then returned to Connor. They didn't need to say anything for Caleb to know they weren't happy.

Being part of a crowd, no matter how small, wasn't the best situation to be in.

The elevator doors pinged open and everyone jostled inside. Caleb's appointment was on the second floor. When the doors opened, he squeezed out of the elevator with Jeremy and Connor and walked toward his doctor's outpatient clinic.

As they walked down the corridor, Caleb checked the layout against the map he'd seen this morning. While his bodyguards sat in the waiting area, he would see the doctor, then head toward the nearest exit. With any luck, he'd be at least thirty minutes away from the hospital before anyone realized he was gone.

His only concern was Sam. If either Jeremy or Connor called her, she might guess where he was going. If that happened, she could arrive at his house about the same time he did. And if she realized what he was doing, she wouldn't have any choice but to do what she'd been trained to do. To stop him—using any means necessary.

SAM GROANED and rolled over in bed. She desperately needed more sleep, but she'd spent the last hour tossing and turning. If she wasn't uneasy about Caleb's appointment in Polson before seeing today's email, she was now. Jeremy and Connor hadn't said much when she showed them the photo, but she knew them well enough to know they were concerned about Caleb's safety.

Fletcher Security and the FBI was doing everything they could to find the man who'd been kidnapped. Sam could only guess at how Anthony's family was feeling. Knowing the person you loved was being tortured by a ruthless terrorist organization was beyond what most people had to endure.

She turned over her pillow and flopped into the soft downy filling. She stared at the ceiling for a few more minutes before deciding to get up. Lying here, imagining what was happening in Polson, wasn't helping anyone. Throwing off the blankets, she slid out of bed and thought about what she had to do today.

Her thick red socks muffled the sound of her footsteps as she gathered her clothes together. Everyone should be back from Polson by eleven o'clock. Before they arrived, she'd call John, ask him if there was any update on Anthony.

She couldn't tell Caleb about his friend. Not yet. Like everyone else, he was getting frustrated at the amount of time it was taking to find the Al-Nusra terrorist cell. If he knew about the kidnapping, he might take matters into his own hands.

Just as she was heading into the bathroom, her cell phone rang. It was Jeremy. "Hi. Are you leaving Polson?"

"Caleb has gone. He left the hospital about thirty-five minutes ago."

"What do you mean *gone*? Weren't you with him?"

"After he had his stitches removed, he left through a door in the staff area. We checked the hospital's security footage. He was on his own. Has anyone emailed him while we've been here?"

Sam rushed across to her laptop. Her cell phone hadn't warned her that Caleb had received another email, but she might have had more sleep than she thought. "I'm checking his emails now."

She ran her eyes down the messages. Nothing new had arrived from the terrorist group. "There's nothing in his emails that we should be worried about. Apart from the doctor, did he talk to anyone else at the hospital?"

"Not that we saw. Why do you think he left?" Jeremy sounded out of breath.

"Are you running?"

"I am. Connor and I are almost at the parking lot."

"He's probably as worried as we are about what's happening. Did he tell the doctor where he was going?"

"The only thing they discussed was his arm."

Another thought crossed Sam's mind. She opened his sent email and groaned.

"What is it?" Jeremy asked.

"You need to get back to the ranger's house. Caleb emailed the terrorist cell. He's giving them the program."

Jeremy cursed. "Connor will call John while I'm driving. We'll ask him to contact the FBI."

Sam threw on her clothes. "I should be able to stop him

before he reaches his property. If John hears anything, ask him to call me straight away."

"Okay. I'll text you as soon as we arrive at Caleb's house."

With a sick feeling in her stomach, Sam ended the call. She hoped Caleb knew what he was doing. Once the FBI arrived, they wouldn't be interested in why he was meeting the Al-Nusra Nuclei. He was about to commit an act of cyberterrorism and he would be treated like a criminal.

CALEB STOPPED his truck in front of his house and ran inside. As he'd driven along the steep and winding road from Sapphire Bay, he'd prayed that he wouldn't meet Sam. What he was doing was dangerous. If she became involved he would have one more person to worry about. One more life hanging in the balance because of a program that was supposed to save lives.

He started the computer that was still in his office. Hidden amongst files on his cloud stage account was the program the terrorists wanted.

Wiping his brow, he copied the information onto an external hard drive and unplugged it from his computer. He had the program, now he had to protect himself. With a trembling hand he opened the bottom drawer of his desk. The extra gun and ammunition wouldn't save his life, but it might give him a few more minutes to get away. He had no idea what he was walking into or how many people would be waiting for him.

In twenty minutes, he was meeting the terrorists in front of the ranger's house. He had chosen the location because it was away from the main road and would take the FBI longer to get to. And he'd need every extra minute he could scrape together.

His plan was simple.

Meet the terrorists. Give them the program. Leave.

Nothing was ever that easy and lots of things could go wrong—including being killed. But if someone didn't do something, they would continue to hurt anyone associated with the EMP project.

With the hard drive in his hand, he rushed into the garage. When Gabe lent him his snowmobile, it wasn't meant to be a getaway vehicle. But it was the safest, quickest, and most reliable way he had of traveling in and out of the clearing.

With a pounding heart, he opened the garage door. It would take fifteen minutes to drive to the ranger's house. Fifteen minutes of second-guessing what he was about to do. And hoping he was still alive at the end of it.

CALEB SLOWED the snowmobile to a crawl and peered around the clearing. The ranger's house looked just as forlorn as the day he'd first seen it with Sam. Even though it looked as though it wouldn't last another winter, he was profoundly grateful it was there. Without its shelter, and the supplies Sam had left inside, he would have died. He only hoped he didn't have to use them again.

He swung his leg over the seat of the snowmobile and stood perfectly still. If the people he was meeting were here, he couldn't see or hear them. Silence echoed through the forest as loudly as the battle cry of a Highland clan.

Taking a deep breath, he unzipped his jacket and braced his arms on either side of his thighs. One of his guns dug into his back. The other was strapped to his hip. Both were loaded and ready to fire.

The sound of engines cut through the heavy silence. He

couldn't tell which direction the noise was coming from. The snow-covered pine trees bounced sound around the clearing like an ancient Greek theater.

Three snowmobiles emerged from behind some trees. They stopped about thirty feet in front of the ranger's house.

Caleb's eyes widened. Slouched behind one of the drivers was a person with a brown sack covering their head. He'd seen TV images of hostages, gagged and blindfolded, but he'd never seen anything like it in real life.

When the driver dismounted, the person fell forward. Caleb didn't know whether it was from sheer exhaustion or because their hands were tied. But either way, they didn't move.

Even in the bitter cold, sweat ran down his back. He wanted to rush across the clearing and help them, but he had to wait. One wrong move and everything could end in disaster.

When all three drivers took off their helmets, Caleb clenched his fists. The fresh-faced, boy-next-door men were nothing like the people he was expecting to see. They looked like college graduates instead of the violent criminals they'd become.

A blond-haired man stepped forward. He couldn't have been more than twenty-five years old. "Do you have the program?"

Was that a Canadian accent? If they'd crossed the border, the FBI would have access to their personal information. All Caleb needed was a license plate number and the FBI could identify them.

He held the hard drive above his head. "It's here." If he was terrified of this meeting, the men opposite him didn't seem worried at all. The smug look they exchanged told him they hadn't imagined getting anything other than what they wanted.

They were too confident, too used to getting their own way. With any luck, by the end of the day, they'd regret ever meeting him.

Caleb nodded toward the snowmobile. "Who did you bring with you?"

The driver with dark brown hair looked over his shoulder, dismissing the person with a careless shrug. "Consider him our parting gift to you."

The blond guy yanked the person off the snowmobile. "Bring the program over here or your friend dies."

Caleb's heart pounded. For a moment he thought the terrorist was holding Sam. But the shape of the person's body was all wrong. He was male and no doubt terrified of what was happening.

The last thing Caleb wanted was to get closer to the terrorists. If he stepped away from his snowmobile, he would be vulnerable. But without backup, he had no choice but to do what they wanted.

"What guarantee do I have that you're not going to shoot me before you leave?"

"You don't get any guarantees." The blond guy pushed his prisoner face down into the snow.

The muffled groan coming from the person's throat made Caleb's stomach twist. Whoever was under the sack was hurt. It would slow him down, slow them both down when they needed to run. Everything had just gone from bad to worse.

With no other option, Caleb took a step forward, then another. To his relief, one of the terrorists pulled the prisoner to his feet and marched him across the clearing. Finally, the odds of leaving here alive were getting better.

When they were no more than ten feet apart, the man held out his hand. "If the program doesn't work, we know where to find you."

Caleb gave him the hard drive. "It works. Once this is over, I don't want to hear from you again."

The terrorist pushed the hostage onto the ground. "If I were you, I'd be careful what you wished for. If this isn't the program, the email I sent this morning is only the beginning. Next time, we won't be so gentle with your colleagues."

Caleb had no idea what he was talking about. He'd come here to give the terrorists the program. If he could help someone else, it was an unexpected bonus.

He studied the men standing beside their snowmobiles. Their guns were pointed straight at him. Caleb kept his hand away from his holster.

"Smart move."

He was outnumbered. Doing anything to annoy the man in front of him wasn't Caleb's intention. The terrorists had the program, now it was time to leave.

One of the men fired a shot into the air.

Caleb flinched as the sound of the bullet echoed around the clearing.

He was in trouble now.

CHAPTER 14

*S*am crouched beside a boulder. She didn't notice the cold wind or last night's full, round moon still hovering in the sky. All she knew was someone had fired a gun and she needed to find Caleb. Fast.

When she'd arrived at Caleb's house, she'd swapped her truck for a set of cross-country skis. The only other vehicles in the garage were the four-wheelers. Taking one of them into the forest would be like signing her own death warrant. The engine was too loud and she could get stuck in the snow.

She checked her watch. It had taken longer than she thought to ski here, but Caleb could still be at the ranger's house. But where were the terrorists and who had fired the gun?

She moved farther into the forest. There was so much about this situation that didn't make sense. The terrorist cell seemed to know what was happening almost as quickly as Caleb and his boss did. Someone must be working for them in the Department of Defense or in the project team.

Taking a deep breath, she pushed forward. The skis

swished through the snow. She found a rhythm, bowed her head, and kept going.

When Sam was a few hundred feet from the house, she unclipped the skis and hid behind some trees.

Was that someone's voice? The sound was muffled, almost incoherent as it bounced around the mountains.

Pulling out her gun, she peered around the trees.

Caleb stood in the clearing, watching three men mount their snowmobiles. Why wasn't he moving?

The men revved their engines and quickly drove away, spewing a trail of snow high into the air.

As Sam rushed forward, Caleb dropped to his knees, untying something that was lying in the snow.

She stumbled, falling head-first onto the icy ground. Pulling herself upright, she looked around the clearing. If the terrorists came back, they'd both be dead.

"Caleb! What are you doing?"

He spun around, his gun pointed straight at her. Shock replaced the anger on his face. "What are you doing here?"

"It doesn't matter. We need to leave. If the terrorists come back they could—"

"They won't come back."

Sam frowned. "You can't know that."

He turned his back on her and leaned down, cradling something in the snow.

She ran forward, skidding to a stop beside him. The bloody body lying in the snow could only be one person. Anthony Sorenson.

She buried the fear rising inside her and swung the backpack off her shoulders. They had to keep Anthony warm until a rescue team arrived. She handed Caleb a survival blanket. "Wrap this around Anthony. I'll get the trauma kit from inside the house and call 9-1-1."

Caleb's eyes widened. "How did you know—"

"I'll be back soon." There would be time later for explanations. Right now, they needed to keep Anthony alive.

CALEB WRAPPED the survival blanket tightly around his friend's body. With trembling hands, he took off his own ski cap and gently pulled it over Anthony's head. "Hang in there, buddy. It will be okay." Anthony mumbled something and Caleb leaned forward. "What did you say?"

"Call Lou."

Caleb wiped the tears out of his eyes. "I'll call her now." Louise was Anthony's wife. They'd been through so much over the last few years that it was hard to imagine how she must be feeling. He pulled out his satellite phone, hoping he still had Anthony's number in his contacts list.

The whop-whop of helicopter blades sounded overhead. Caleb looked into the sky. The rescue team must have been in the area to be here so quickly. But it wasn't the Search and Rescue Team. It was the FBI.

"Put your hands in the air and move away from the body."

The voice echoing from the helicopter's loud speaker filled Caleb with dread. He did as he was told. If they knew he was here, then they probably knew what he'd done.

Sam ran out of the ranger's house. When she saw the helicopter, she stopped. Instead of rushing forward to give him the trauma kit, she pulled out her satellite phone. While she was speaking, the helicopter landed beside the house.

Within seconds, the chopper doors opened and six FBI special agents ran toward Caleb. As soon as he saw their body armor and assault weapons, he knew he wouldn't be going anywhere except into an interrogation room.

He looked at Sam. The terrorists would escape if someone didn't get to a computer soon. "I added a tracking code into the EMP program," he yelled. "There's a safe in my office. The code to opening it is my satellite phone number. A red book contains all the information you'll need to log into my account."

Sam dropped the trauma kit onto the ground. "You gave the program to the terrorists?"

"It was the only way I could get them to leave everyone alone. But it's not what you think. There's a—"

Six FBI special agents pointed their guns at Caleb.

"Stop talking," one of the men yelled. "You're coming with us."

Sam moved quickly. "Call Special Agent William Parker," she told the agents. "Caleb Andrews isn't the person you should be arresting."

Caleb looked at Anthony, then back at the special agents. "My friend needs a doctor."

"Drop the phone and get on your knees," yelled one of the agents. "We're taking you into Polson for questioning."

"Don't worry about Anthony," Sam assured him. "I'll make sure he's taken to the hospital."

Caleb looked into her eyes. "You need to activate the tracking code before it's too late."

Sam nodded and backed away.

Two agents walked toward him. He was in deep trouble.

As Caleb boarded the helicopter, the last thing he saw was an agent kneeling beside Anthony, and Sam leaving on his snowmobile. He knew that activating the code wasn't enough. Someone had to use the data to find the terrorists. Otherwise, the FBI might never see them again.

≈

SAM PACED BACKWARD AND FORWARD. In the time it had taken her to drive to Caleb's house, the FBI had flown him to Polson. John Fletcher, her boss, had met him there.

She'd found the notebook Caleb had told her about. Thanks to his tracking code, they'd not only followed the EMP program to the American base, but to what appeared to be the Al-Nusra's main headquarters. Six hours later, a joint operation between the police, the FBI, and the CIA was underway. Two warehouses, one in Chicago and another in Erbil, the capital of Iraqi Kurdistan, were about to be raided.

Sam leaned forward, staring at the live images on her computer screen. What she saw was replicated on computers in Washington, D.C., Chicago, and Erbil.

"We have units moving into place," the special agent sitting in Chicago said.

"Erbil is good to go," another voice repeated over the speakerphone.

On one side of the screen, FBI special agents took position around a large brick building on the outskirts of Chicago. On the other, images from a body camera showed CIA operatives moving toward a building in the center of Erbil.

It was two o'clock in the morning in Iraq. Early enough, she hoped, that any civilian causalities would be minimized.

She still couldn't believe Caleb had given the EMP program to the terrorists. Even with the tracking device, he'd traded the threat to a few people's lives for the well-being of millions. She couldn't blame him for feeling personally responsible for the safety of his friends and family. But she was angry that he hadn't talked to her before making the decision to commit cyberterrorism. It didn't matter how well-meaning his intentions were, a judge wouldn't treat his case any differently from the people who had threatened him.

Jeremy handed her a cup of coffee. "Drink this. I added extra sugar."

Sam took a sip and winced at the sweetness. She was tired, but not tired enough to drink the thick, hot liquid that Jeremy had made. "Thanks. I can definitely taste the sugar."

He frowned when she left the cup on the desk. "I spoke to John a few minutes ago. Caleb is able to come home. The FBI isn't charging him with anything."

She took a deep, shaky breath, releasing some of the tension she'd been holding onto. For most of the night, she'd deliberately focused on tracking the program and not what was happening in Polson. "That's great news."

"Counting down. One minute," the voice in Erbil said.

Sam crossed her fingers, hoping no one got hurt.

"Thirty seconds."

She studied the images, looking for any sign that the agents were walking into a trap.

"Go."

Agents swarmed the buildings in both cities, searching for anyone connected to the terrorist organization.

Flashes of light filled the screen in Erbil. Gunfire. Loud, nonstop, and deadly. She held her breath as people yelled and screamed.

The agents in both cities moved with purpose, sweeping through the buildings like the worst storm imaginable.

For a brief moment, Sam closed her eyes. She'd seen a lot of field operations while she was in the Army. When military personnel got to this point, it was a combination of skill, gut instinct, and sheer luck that brought them home uninjured. And sometimes, that luck ran out.

Jeremy's hand landed on her shoulder. "Have another sip of coffee."

She looked into his dark brown eyes and sighed. That sounded like a really good idea.

∽

CALEB WALKED into his home and closed the front door. He could hear voices coming from his office, the sound of someone loading the dishwasher in the kitchen.

It felt surreal to be standing here, in the place that was supposed to be his sanctuary, after being interrogated for seven hours. When he'd left the police station with John and his lawyer, he was exhausted.

They'd gone back to a hotel to regroup and make sense of everything that had happened. Afterward, Caleb had stood under a scalding hot shower, washing the worry and stress from his body. By the time he returned to the main living area, John had ordered room service and Caleb was feeling less like a criminal.

He could see why Sam enjoyed working at Fletcher Security. John knew next to nothing about him, but he'd dropped everything to fly with his lawyer to Polson and sit with him while the FBI did what they were paid to do.

A noise made him jump, yanking his mind back to the here and now.

Sam stopped in the middle of the hallway. Her eyes widened and her expression became guarded. "Welcome back. I didn't think you'd be home tonight."

"John wanted me to stay in Polson, but I wouldn't have slept." He took off his jacket and hung it over the coat stand. He didn't know how to fill the awkward silence stretching between them.

Sam looked through the glass panel beside the front door. "Is John with you?"

"No. He flew back to Bozeman with his lawyer."

Not even a flicker of surprise crossed Sam's face. She must be used to her boss jetting in and out of airports.

She crossed her arms in front of her chest. "Jeremy and

Connor are here. Two FBI special agents left about five minutes ago."

There could have been a party in his living room for all Caleb cared. He was tired and needed to sleep. "I'll see you in the morning."

Sam's arms dropped to her sides. "Wait. What about your friend? How is he?"

"Anthony has a fractured cheekbone and lots of cuts and bruises, but he'll be okay. The doctors want him to stay in Polson Hospital for a few nights."

"Is someone looking after him?"

"The FBI is guarding him. His wife will be there first thing in the morning."

"That's good. How are you?"

"Tired. I'm going to bed." He turned and lifted his foot onto the staircase.

"You can't. We haven't talked about what happened."

Caleb could barely string two words together. "I was interrogated for nearly seven hours. I'm happy to talk about what happened tomorrow, but not now."

"Why did you give the terrorists the program?"

He pinched the bridge of his nose. "Not now, Sam. I'm too tired."

She took a step forward. "I need to tell you what I did."

"You activated the tracking software."

"I did more than that."

Caleb had no idea what was coming next, but it must be serious for Sam to look so worried.

"While we were working together, I created a gateway into your program. All copies of the program have been destroyed, except for the ones in Washington, D.C."

Caleb's mouth dropped open. "What?"

"After we found the Al-Nusra cells, I activated a virus. The terrorists' copies of the EMP program won't work."

He took a deep breath, fighting to keep his pounding heart under control. "You were supposed to help me, not sabotage my work. You had no right to release a virus into the program."

Sam lifted her chin. "I was helping you."

"You destroyed the program!"

"The only copies that are destroyed are the ones that shouldn't have been shared in the first place."

Something inside of him snapped. He'd trusted her. Letting her work on the program was a mistake. Falling in love with her was an even bigger one. How could he have been so stupid?

"Did you ever consider that I might have safeguards in place to protect the program? And just maybe, if I knew half as much about programming as you think I do, that I'd have a double-safeguard ready to use?"

"You were being interrogated. The FBI wouldn't have let you release a virus when they didn't know if they could trust you."

Caleb's heart pounded. "And you'd know all about trust," he ground out. "First thing in the morning, I want you, Connor, and Jeremy to leave." He gripped the bannister, holding onto it like a lifeline. "I'm going to bed."

Sam's white face stared back at him. "It's not what you think."

She was wrong. He knew exactly what she'd done, and he wouldn't let her close enough to hurt him again.

CHAPTER 15

That night, Sam hardly slept. If Caleb's anger wasn't enough to cope with, her PTSD had raised its ugly head. The more she tried to identify the trigger, the worse it became. So much had happened over the last twenty-four hours that she was struggling to make sense of anything.

By four o'clock the next morning, she'd packed her suitcase and was ready to leave. The chance of bumping into Caleb was slim, but she hadn't wanted to risk it. So she stayed in her room, reading some reports her team had sent her. If someone had asked her what the reports were about, she couldn't have told them. But at least it helped reduce her anxiety and stopped some of her tears from falling.

When she heard Caleb leave, she made her way downstairs. Thankfully, by seven o'clock, Connor and Jeremy were ready to drive back to Bozeman.

The last thing she had to do was return Caleb's satellite phone. She walked into his office and looked at the bare walls. With a heavy heart, she remembered the photos of his project team. The maps, the random sheets of paper, and the color-coded lines on the whiteboard that had given the room character.

It was like standing in a living room after the Christmas tree had been taken down. The office felt cold and empty, as if the heart of the room had disappeared along with the things that made it special.

She placed the satellite phone on Caleb's desk and hoped that one day, he would forgive her.

"Are you ready?" Jeremy stood in the doorway, concern etched into the hard lines of his face.

She forced a smile. "Just about. I want to leave a note for Caleb."

"Do you think that's a good idea?"

Sam didn't know anymore. Jeremy had told her that Caleb had gone back to the ranger's house, leaving them to pack their belongings and head home.

She took a deep breath, pushing at the black walls trying to suffocate her. Hurting Caleb had never been her intention. She was sent here to do a job. She'd done it, but it came at a cost she'd never expected.

Tears filled her eyes. "It seems wrong to leave without saying goodbye."

Jeremy stared at her for a few seconds before walking across the room. He opened his arms and Sam stepped into his tight embrace. "I know your PTSD is back. You'll be okay. Connor and I will look after you."

The walls she was trying to hold up, crumbled. She sobbed into Jeremy's shoulder, letting go of everything that was wrong in her life. When the worst of her tears had passed, she took a deep, shuddering breath and stepped away.

Jeremy reached for something on the desk. "You'd better use these."

A box of tissues landed in her hands. She forced a smile,

wanting him to know how much his kindness meant to her. "Thank you."

"You're welcome. We're having lunch at Pastor Steven's house tomorrow. You should come."

Sam wasn't the only person with PTSD. Jeremy and Connor had learned how to live with their symptoms. Along with eight other men and women, they regularly went to Pastor Steven's support group. She'd gone to a few meetings when she'd first arrived in Bozeman, but she hadn't been back in months.

"Lunch sounds like a good idea." She blew her nose and took a deep breath. "You're right about the note to Caleb. Some things are better left unsaid." There would be plenty of time to think about what had happened later. Right now, she needed to go home and reset her life.

With shaking hands, she zipped up her jacket. "Okay. Let's go." And after one last look around the office, she left.

TWO DAYS LATER, Sam frowned at the report John gave her. "This can't be right."

"The FBI is analyzing what's left of the program. The document you're holding contains their interim findings. The virus you uploaded didn't destroy the program. Someone else's did. It looks as though there was more to the tracking software than we thought."

"Caleb said he had safeguards that would stop the terrorists from using the program. But he would have needed access to a computer to release the virus."

"Not necessarily."

There were other options, but she doubted he would have used them. Especially when his team was still working on the program. "Even if the virus was released using a time-delay sequence, it might not have helped. No one knew where the terrorists were based. The FBI and the CIA might not have been able to arrest them before the program was destroyed."

"Caleb would have considered that outcome before he installed the virus."

No matter what John said, Caleb wasn't reckless. She turned to the next page of the report. "Who had access to the program before Caleb sent the final copy to Washington, D.C.?"

"You and the chairperson of the project."

Sam flipped to the front of the document. Something about Caleb's boss hadn't felt right from the moment she'd seen his photo. But nothing about Richard Lee's life had raised red flags with anyone. Except her.

"Do we know anything about Richard apart from what Fletcher Security and the FBI identified in their report?"

"No."

Sam tapped her fingers against the arm of the chair. "Where is his ex-wife?"

"I don't know. What are you thinking?"

"The Al-Nusra tried to kidnap Caleb's sister. What if they'd threatened Richard's ex-wife, too? Even if they'd had a horrible divorce, no one would let a terrorist group hurt someone, especially if they could stop it."

"Richard would have said something if that had happened. The FBI or another company could have provided his ex-wife with personal protection."

John sat back in his chair. "Regardless of who's involved, we don't have to worry. The FBI and the CIA are continuing the investigation. It's time to walk away."

Sam didn't often feel frustrated, but she really wanted to know who had destroyed the program.

"How are you feeling?"

She'd told John her PTSD was back. After this meeting,

she was taking two weeks off work. "A little better. I went to Pastor Steven's support group yesterday. It helped a lot. And one of the PTSD therapists can see me this afternoon at the hospital."

"That's good. You know I'm here for you. If you need anything, let me know."

Tears filled Sam's eyes. "Thank you. Jeremy and Connor have been wonderful. I don't know what I would have done without them."

"They know what you're going through. How was Caleb when you left?"

"I don't know. He went back to the ranger's house." She took a deep breath, readying herself for what she would say. "When he came back from Polson, I told him I'd uploaded a virus into the program. He wasn't happy."

John's gaze sharpened. "I don't imagine he was. Why did you tell him?"

"I didn't want him to find out from someone else. He trusted me with the program and he feels as though I let him down."

"Did you tell him the Department of Defense told you to install the virus?"

Sam shook her head. "It doesn't matter how it happened or that it wasn't my virus that destroyed the program. I went behind his back and added something to the program that he didn't know about." After leaving Sapphire Bay, the only thing she knew for certain was that Caleb would never trust her again. So many people in his life had let him down, and now she was one of them.

John didn't ask any more questions about Caleb. Instead, he handed her a folder. "I spoke to a friend in the Department of Defense this morning. He was impressed with your work on the EMP project. It looks as though we'll be doing a lot more work for the government."

Sam opened the folder. Inside were the schematics for a new surveillance drone her team had designed. "Does this mean what I think it does?"

John nodded. "They liked your team's presentation. They want to finance the development of the prototype. If it meets their requirements, they'll approve the second phase of the contract."

"Full production?"

John's smile gave her the answer she was hoping for.

Her team would be super excited. They'd spent months developing a camera that was no bigger than a pea. Sitting on top of a drone the size of a wasp, its range, accuracy, and picture quality was unbeatable.

"That's the best news I've had for a while."

John's smile dimmed. "It will get better, Sam."

"I know. It just takes time. Thanks for taking care of Caleb in Polson. I'm sure he appreciated everything you did."

"He was more worried about you." John's eyes softened. "I know I always talk about keeping our emotions out of our work, but sometimes it's hard. From what I saw of Caleb, he's a good person."

Sam nodded. He was more than good. He was the best person she'd ever met.

"Don't be too hard on yourself or him. Once the FBI has finished their investigation, I'm sure they'll find a number of security issues with the EMP project."

Sam sighed. John knew more than he was telling her, but that was okay. After today's meeting, she would leave the fate of the EMP project in someone else's hands.

CALEB GAVE SHERLOCK, Gabe's large German Shepherd, a big hug. "What would I do without you?"

"It can't be that bad," Gabe said from the doorway. "What's happened? You sounded stressed on the phone."

"I gave the terrorists a copy of the EMP program."

Gabe's hand froze on the zipper of his jacket. "You did what?"

"It was the first version I sent through to the Pentagon. I hid tracking software inside the coding. It shows the location of the program, no matter where it's sent."

"Are you crazy? You could have been arrested or killed."

"Someone had to stop the terrorists."

"But did it have to be you?"

"No one had a better plan." Caleb headed toward the kitchen. Sherlock and Gabe followed. He knew he'd taken a huge risk, but he'd made sure no one would be able to use the program. "After the terrorist cells were located, I was supposed to destroy the program."

"What happened?"

Caleb handed Gabe one of the toasted sandwiches he'd cooked a few minutes earlier. "The FBI took me into Polson for questioning. I was being interrogated and couldn't upload the virus."

"I'm almost too scared to ask, but what happened to the program?"

"It was destroyed. But not by me."

Gabe patted Sherlock's head. "Was it Sam?"

Caleb's eyebrows rose. "Why would you say that?"

"She works for one of the best security companies in the country. If she thought there was any chance you'd hand over the program, she would have taken steps to stop you."

"It wasn't Sam. It was my boss, Richard Lee. If I couldn't release the virus, I needed someone I could trust to do it."

"If Sam didn't harm the program, why are you so upset?"

Caleb frowned. "Because she tried to destroy the program

with her own virus. It didn't work because Richard had already launched his."

Gabe bit into one of the sandwiches. "Did you expect anything else? She's ex-Army. Most of the people I've met from the military have a sixth sense when it comes to trouble. That's what makes them good at their job. Sit down and eat something. You're making me nervous."

Caleb sat beside his friend. "I thought I could trust her."

"What are you more upset about? The fact that she planted a virus in the program or that she didn't tell you what she was doing?"

"If she was worried about the program, she could have talked to me."

"Would you have told her what you were doing?"

"Probably not. I didn't want her to get hurt."

Gabe stopped chewing. "I thought you'd sent the program over the Internet. What actually happened?"

"I met three of the terrorists at the ranger's house. I copied the program onto an external hard drive and gave it to them. I didn't realize they had a hostage with them. I still don't know how Anthony was kidnapped."

Gabe's eyes widened. "You aren't joking, are you?"

Caleb shook his head. "I wish I was. I'm visiting Anthony tomorrow. Hopefully, he can tell me what happened."

"So where does Sam fit into all of this?"

"Nowhere. She went back to Bozeman."

"And?"

"And nothing." Caleb refused to believe that Sam had created the gateway into his program out of concern for him. There had to be more to it than that.

"I thought you liked her?"

"I did. But feelings can change, especially when you realize the person you fell in love with doesn't exist."

Gabe pushed away his plate. "Sam is human, just like the rest of us. Have you talked to her about what happened?"

"No."

"Well, while you're thinking about whether that's a good idea, I'll make coffee."

With Gabe on the other side of the kitchen, Sherlock turned to Caleb. His big chocolate-brown eyes pleaded with him for a treat. Before Gabe came back, Caleb took some melted cheese out of his sandwich and gave it to him.

"I saw that," Gabe said with a smile. "It's just as well your arm is healing. Otherwise, Sherlock would be pulling you outside for a game of fetch."

Caleb looked through the kitchen window and sighed. A game of fetch was exactly what he needed, especially after the last couple of days.

❧

"Don't worry about Caleb." Shelley draped her arm around Sam's shoulders. "We have each other and that's all that matters."

"Oh, please," Bailey said. "That's what everyone says and it makes no difference."

"Of course, it makes a difference. It's good to know that someone cares."

Bailey picked up a bowling ball. "Talking about people caring, I saw your ex-fiancé last week. He looked remarkably unscathed for someone who was dumped at the altar."

Shelley sat ramrod straight. "I broke off our engagement the day before we got married."

"The *night* before you got married."

"It's better than calling off the marriage on the day of the wedding," Shelley said with a sigh. "It wasn't the best timing

I've ever had, but at least I didn't marry him for the wrong reasons."

"Exactly," Sam said. "You made a decision and followed through. That's all anyone can ask."

Shelley and Bailey looked at each other.

"Is that what happened to you?" Bailey asked.

Sam wanted to tell her sisters exactly what had happened, but she couldn't. She was paid to help Caleb with his program, not tell her family what he was doing. "You'd better hit the pins," she said to Bailey. "Shelley is still ahead by four shots."

With more skill than half the people around them, Bailey pulled back her arm and fired the bowling ball down the alley.

Within seconds, the ball slammed into the front pin. Flashes of white filled the alley as all the pins flew into the air.

Shelley held her hand over her mouth. "Oh my, goodness. Where did you learn to do that?"

"Boyfriend number four. He was the state tenpin bowling champion three years in a row."

Sam frowned. "I didn't know you'd dated a bowler."

"That's because you were too busy building gadgets in your workshop. He was a nice guy, but he spent most of his life at the bowling alley. It's hard to compete with a set of pins."

"There are worse things in life," Shelley said dryly. "Try living up to a potential mother-in-law's standards."

Sam looked closely at Shelley. "Is that what happened?"

Shelley picked up her ball. "It was only part of the problem. The other part was me."

Bailey patted her sister on the back. "There's nothing wrong with wanting something more. Too many people settle for what's comfortable."

Sam smiled at her sisters. "And the Jones family don't settle. Ever."

Shelley slid her fingers into the ball. "You might regret saying that."

Bailey groaned. "She's going for a strike. You could have talked about settling when it was your turn, Sam."

"But it wouldn't have had the same effect." Shelley did her unique seven-step shuffle toward the alley, pulled back her arm, and gracefully spun the ball toward the pins.

"She's going to do it," Bailey screeched. "There goes my winning meal at Charlie's Bar and Grill."

When the pins went flying, Shelley threw her arms in the air and danced a happy jig. "I did it. I did it. That's two games in a row. Who is the champion?"

Sam dropped her head to her chest. "You are the champion. But it wouldn't hurt to have a little humility."

"I agree," Bailey said. "Especially if your opponents are paying for your meal."

"Sisters are never on the opposite team. They always have your back, even when you don't think they're there."

Sam looked at Shelley. Something she'd read in the report about the EMP project stuck in her mind. Richard Lee, the chairperson of the project, had two young daughters. What if they were the missing link?

"Are you okay?" Bailey asked. "You're a million miles away."

Sam looked at the time. "I need to make a phone call."

Shelley sighed. "Why do I have a feeling we'll be ordering takeout?"

"Maybe because that's what always happens," Bailey said unhappily. "The phone call turns into a quick meeting, and the quick meeting turns into a three-hour ordeal. By that time, no one wants to go anywhere."

Sam studied her sisters' disappointed faces. "Okay. I get it.

None of us are settling for second best. But this is really important."

Shelley held out her wrist. "You can make the call, but I'm timing you. You have two minutes."

Two minutes was all it would take. Sam pulled out her cell phone and called her boss's number. John still had people he could speak to in the FBI. At least if he told someone, they could make sure Richard Lee's daughters were not in danger.

As it turned out, it took less than a minute to tell him what was worrying her.

After she ended the call, she smiled at her sisters. "I told you it wouldn't take long."

Bailey frowned. "Why are you worried about someone's daughters?"

Sam's smile slipped. "It's part of a case I was working on. John will make sure they're okay."

"Are you sure?" Shelley asked. "Because we could get takeout if you need more time."

"They don't live in Bozeman but thanks for understanding. Does anyone want to play another game?"

Bailey's worried frown turned into a grin. "No, but I know somewhere that sells the best spareribs in Montana."

Shelley rubbed her hands together. "Charlie's Bar and Grill, here we come!"

CHAPTER 16

Three weeks later, Sam sat at her desk, staring at her computer screen. Even though Fletcher Security wasn't officially involved in the Al-Nusra case, she was curious about what had happened after the raids.

With the approval of her boss, she'd called the FBI's field office in Polson. They wouldn't tell her anything about the terrorist group. She did, however, discover that Special Agent William Parker was still on assignment. She hoped that meant he was with Caleb's sister, but she just didn't know.

She opened another tab on her computer screen and searched for news articles about the raids on the buildings in Iraq and Chicago. Nothing. It was as if a big black hole had split the world in half and no one was saying anything.

Hailey, her personal assistant, stood in the doorway. "Caleb Andrews is here to see you. He's not listed on your meeting schedule."

Sam's eyes widened. Caleb was the last person she'd expected to see.

"Sam?"

She blinked, then focused on Hailey. "Sorry. It's okay. I'll go and see what he wants. Is he in the lobby?"

"He is. Are you feeling all right?"

If you didn't count a pounding heart and sweaty palms, she was fine. "I'll be back in about twenty minutes. If anyone wants me, they can call me on my cell phone."

As she walked downstairs, Sam tried to imagine why Caleb was here. He wouldn't have come to Bozeman unless it was important. Something must have happened to his sister. It was the most logical explanation for his unplanned visit. But if that were the case, he could have called Fletcher Security instead of driving for four hours.

Before she stepped into the lobby, Sam took a deep breath, straightened her skirt, and walked calmly down the main staircase. The Jones family didn't settle for second best. And Caleb Andrews, for all his wonderful qualities, would always be second best if he couldn't trust her.

WHILE HE WAITED for Sam's personal assistant, Caleb flicked through a magazine, hoping it would calm his nerves. He wished he was feeling as confident as the receptionist who'd greeted him. Even though what Sam had done was wrong, he'd acted like an idiot. Being angry with her wouldn't make any difference to what had happened. And staying angry at her wouldn't achieve anything.

When he'd booked his flights to Washington, D.C., stopping in Bozeman had seemed like a good idea. Now that he was here, he wasn't so sure.

He would understand if Sam didn't want to see him. She had staff who depended on her and work she needed to do. But two months ago, despite her workload and her sister's wedding, she'd traveled to Sapphire Bay to help him. If nothing else, she deserved an apology and his thanks.

Caleb's gaze was caught by the woman walking across the lobby. It had only been three weeks since he'd last seen Sam, but it felt like a lifetime. He'd missed spending time with her. It didn't matter whether they were working through the complex code he'd created or enjoying dinner together. Her kindness and sense of humor made him feel complete.

Her eyes locked on his and he could have sworn he felt the earth move.

"Hi, Caleb. I didn't expect to see you again." Sam clasped her hands in front of her skirt.

Her steady gaze worried him. He must have really hurt her. "I'm on my way to Washington, D.C. I wanted to apologize for what happened. For how I treated you."

Sam stared at him with wary eyes. "Apology accepted. Are you meeting the EMP team?"

"I am. We're working through different deployment options."

"You still have a copy of the program?" Sam seemed surprised.

"The virus didn't destroy the latest version. Our team was back at work the next day, making sure the virus hadn't spread to other software."

"Did it?"

He shook his head. "No, we were lucky." Caleb was sure Sam was getting ready to leave. Not that he blamed her. He wouldn't want to spend time with a person who'd yelled at him, either. "Would you like to go somewhere for coffee?"

For the first time since he'd met her, Sam seemed lost. "Are you okay?"

"I'm fine, but I can't leave. I have a lot of work to do."

"It wouldn't need to be a long coffee break. I have to be at the airport in an hour."

Sam bit her bottom lip. "I don't know if having coffee with you is a good idea."

"I could update you on what's happened since you left Sapphire Bay."

Sam's eyes connected with his. "I've been trying to get an update from the FBI. But because Fletcher Security isn't involved in the project anymore, no one will speak to me."

"I know as much as anyone else. I'm happy to tell you what's happening." He felt like a fraud. Using the EMP project as an excuse to spend time with Sam wasn't only unethical, it was plain stupid.

To his surprise, Sam nodded. "If you're happy to use one of our meeting rooms, we could talk there."

The room Sam took him to wasn't far from where they were standing.

She turned on the coffeepot and sat at a round table. "Have you heard from your sister?"

"She's still being looked after by the FBI. She called me a couple of days ago. She sounds like a nice person." He took off his jacket and draped it over the back of the chair. "Anthony was discharged from Polson Hospital a few days after you left. He's recovering at home."

"That's good. He must be feeling overwhelmed by what happened."

"Having his wife with him makes a big difference." Caleb had visited Anthony twice since he'd left the hospital. It would take him a long time to recover, but he was strong.

Sam rested her elbows on the table. "Two weeks ago, I went out with Shelley and Bailey. They said something about sisters which made me think about Richard Lee's daughters. Do you know if they're safe?"

"They're okay. Is your question related to the virus Richard uploaded to the program?"

Sam's eyebrows rose. "Did he tell you that's what he did?"

"He was my safeguard. If I couldn't get to a computer, he would make sure the program was destroyed."

Sam was shocked. "He knew you were giving the program to the terrorists?"

Caleb nodded. "Their threats were getting worse. The FBI had no idea where they were, so we gave the terrorists what they wanted. Except it wasn't the real program."

"It wasn't?"

"The program the virus infected wouldn't have worked. But it was close enough that a programmer would have been fooled."

Sam rubbed her forehead. "I can't believe Richard was part of your plans. He spoke to me on the night of the raids. He didn't sound upset or more stressed than anyone else."

"Richard watched the live video from his office in Washington, D.C. He knew about the tracking software and how to access the data. When the raid was over, he destroyed the program."

Sam took a deep breath and closed her eyes.

"Are you all right?"

She nodded and sent him a forced smile. "I'll make the coffee."

Something wasn't right, but Caleb didn't know what it was.

When Sam handed him one of the cups, he took it and smiled. "Thank you."

She frowned. "There's something you should know." She placed her cup on the table and sat down. "After the Al-Nusra tried to kidnap your sister, I installed an app on your email account. It redirected your messages to me. I released most of them, but kept anything from the Al-Nusra Nuclei."

Caleb pinched the bridge of his nose. If he thought the day couldn't get any worse, he was wrong. "Are you still checking my emails?"

"No. I turned off the app when I left Sapphire Bay."

He should be annoyed that Sam had deliberately censored his mail, but too much had happened. "Why did you do it?"

"I was worried about you. The Al-Nusra's threats were getting more violent. They were targeting your friends and family, people you cared about. I had to make sure they didn't make you do something you'd regret."

"I guess I did that myself," Caleb muttered. "What emails didn't I see?"

"They sent photos of Anthony while they were torturing him. The other messages contained threats. I don't have access to the messages, but the FBI does."

Caleb cradled his coffee cup. The warmth seeped into his skin and made him feel human. "When I gave the terrorists the program, one of them said something about Anthony. I didn't know what he was talking about. It would have been the photos."

"I'm sorry. I know you don't trust me, but I was there to protect you and the program. Sometimes I had to make decisions you wouldn't like. But I made them because they were the right thing to do."

Something Sam had said made Caleb uneasy. "Who asked you to protect the program?"

For a moment, he didn't think Sam would answer him.

"Who was it, Sam?"

"I don't know their name, but it was someone above your boss. After the death threats your team was receiving, they were worried the program would get into the wrong hands. They gave Fletcher Security the authority to do whatever was necessary to keep you and the program safe."

Caleb didn't know what to say. Every accusation he'd hurled at Sam was based on lies. He thought she'd tried to sabotage the program, but she was doing her job. A job he should have known about.

Sam's cell phone rang. She looked at the caller display and frowned. "I have to answer this. I'll be back soon."

After she left, Caleb stood in front of the window. He'd seriously misjudged her and he didn't know what to do about it.

A few minutes later, Sam walked into the meeting room. "Thanks for waiting."

"It was no problem, but I need to leave."

She sent him another forced smile. "I appreciate your apology. It means a lot."

Caleb's heart pounded. Even when they first met, they hadn't been this unsure of each other. He looked into her eyes and sighed. He wanted to give her a hug, but anything other than a handshake wouldn't feel right.

He extended his hand and hoped that one day, they could be friends. "Thank you for everything you've done. I'm sorry I misjudged you."

Her hand slipped into his and, not for the first time, he wished their lives could have been different.

THIS VISIT TO WASHINGTON, D.C. was one of the hardest Caleb had made. For the last four days, he'd been struggling to keep focused and add value to what the rest of the team were doing. He kept thinking about Sam, about the changes he wanted to make in his life.

Unfortunately, he wasn't the only person having difficulty concentrating. Anthony's kidnapping had made the entire EMP team wary of everything. They'd all taken extra precautions with their safety. Two of the team had moved their families away from Washington, D.C. and others were in the process of hiring bodyguards.

The FBI and the CIA were working hard to identify more

members of the Al-Nusra Nuclei. Whether they could completely eradicate the terrorist cell was anyone's guess.

The unplanned meeting Caleb was about to have with his boss worried him.

Because the team only had a week together, each day ran to a tight schedule. Spur-of-the-moment meetings didn't happen and, when they did, it was because something serious had happened.

He knocked on Richard's office door.

"Come in."

Caleb smiled at his boss. Richard needed something to brighten his day. Sam was right. The terrorists had threatened Richard's daughters. And now, with round-the-clock protection from the FBI, his family were having a hard time rebuilding their lives.

"I got your message. Is everything all right?"

Richard stood and shook his hand. "It could be better. The FBI has given me an update of what's happening with the terrorists. I thought you'd appreciate knowing what's going on."

Caleb sat opposite his boss. "You're not telling the whole team?"

"Not yet. It's not because I don't want to. It's because I don't know who I can trust."

"Has there been another information leak?"

"This one was planned." Richard leaned forward in his chair. "I've been working with the FBI. We planted false information about the project. This morning, a person was arrested and charged with a number of serious offenses."

That wasn't what Caleb was expecting to hear. "Did they work for the Department of Defense?"

"It was worse. They were an FBI Special Agent. It will take a few months to get to the bottom of how much information they stole, but it's not looking good."

"Is that how the terrorists knew where I was living?"

Richard nodded. "All our personnel files, our schedules, our family details, every scrap of information the FBI had about the project was at the agent's disposal. We were lucky no one was killed."

The things that hadn't made sense began to fall into place. The special agent would have known how close they were to making the EMP program work. Kidnapping Anthony, threatening Caleb's sister and Richard's daughters—it was all planned to put the most amount of pressure on them.

"Can you tell me who leaked the information?"

"No, but it isn't any of the agent's you've met."

Caleb breathed a sigh of relief. At least they weren't betrayed by someone working alongside them. "Is the project still going ahead?"

Richard nodded. "The special agent didn't have access to the latest version of the program. With the previous versions destroyed, the project is still a vital factor in our national security. There is some good news." Richard handed him a folder. "Through their intelligence services, two governments heard about what we're doing. They're interested in collaborating in an international roll-out of the software. If their proposal is as good as it seems, we could have the first commercial prototype running within six months. To make that happen, I'll need people on the negotiating team who I can trust. Would you be interested?"

A year ago, Caleb would have given anything to be part of the team. He'd worked with Richard on other negotiations. He was a good man, but every minute of every day would be focused on the program. There would be no time for family or friends.

He looked around Richard's office. There were certificates on the walls, photos with Senators and the President—a lifetime's worth of memories—the kind that used to matter to Caleb. But he didn't want that life. Not anymore.

He took a deep breath, knowing this would be his first step in a new direction. One that he hoped led straight to Sam. "I appreciate your offer, but I can't join your negotiating team. After what's happened, I need to spend more time with the people I love."

Richard sighed. "I understand." He picked up a framed photograph and handed it to Caleb. "These are my girls."

The photo had been taken a few years ago. Stacey, Richard's ex-wife, was cuddling their daughters and laughing at the camera. You could see the joy and happiness on their faces, the contentment that came from knowing they were loved. When Caleb looked back at Richard, there were tears in his eyes.

"That was five years ago. We were happy and in love but, even then, I put my job first. Stacey wanted to spend more time together, but I kept working seventy-hour weeks. I was hardly home and when I was, I was still thinking about work. Stacey was lonely, but I was too caught up in my career to notice. It wasn't until she left that I realized how selfish I'd been."

"Have you told Stacey how you feel?"

Richard shook his head. "It's too late. She fell in love with someone else."

Caleb handed Richard the photo. "I'm sorry."

"Don't make the same mistakes I did. Nothing is worth more than the people you love."

Seeing the sadness on Richard's face made Caleb realize one thing. He didn't belong here. He needed to go back to Bozeman, spend time with Sam and, hopefully, build a new kind of normal with her.

~

"GOLD TINSEL." Elena poured her famous pasta sauce over a layer of lasagna noodles.

Sam picked up her pen. "Are you sure you want tinsel this year? Why not real pine garlands?" For the last half hour, Sam had been making a list of the Christmas decorations her mom wanted to hang in her house.

"I don't mind fresh pine trees but, this year, I want tinsel and lights." Creamy cheese sauce joined the sheets of pasta. "We could always buy the tinsel that has fairy lights in it. Shelley bought some from Murdoch's and they look stunning."

"Murdoch's?" The last time Sam had been in the ranch supply store, she hadn't seen any Christmas decorations. "Are you sure you have the right store?"

"As sure as I'll ever be when your sister tells me something. Remember to compliment Shelley when you see her house. She's spent a fortune on decorations. I think she's compensating for not going through with the wedding."

Sam smiled. "You've been watching too much Dr. Phil. Shelley always goes overboard at Christmas."

"But not like this. The Boy Scouts asked if they could do a tour of her house after their next meeting. Her property is turning into a tourist attraction."

"Maybe that's not a bad thing. It's better than having your name splashed across the Facebook page as a runaway bride."

Elena handed Sam a block of cheese and a grater. "Grate enough cheese to sprinkle over the top of the lasagna."

Since she'd been home, Sam had been learning how to cook. Each recipe was a family favorite. Most of them had been passed down from generation to generation. Along with the cooking lessons, her mom told her stories about her family and where each recipe came from. It was no wonder Shelley and Bailey had enjoyed their time in the kitchen.

"How is that man of yours?"

For a moment, Sam didn't know who her mom was talking about. "Caleb?"

"Is there another man?"

Sam could almost see her mom's grandbaby radar twitching.

"No, and there's no Caleb, either. He's working in Washington, D.C. When he's finished, he'll return to Sapphire Bay."

Elena sighed. "You should start thinking about your future. Your dad and I aren't getting any younger. By the time you and your sisters have children, we'll be too old to enjoy them."

Sam couldn't see that happening anytime soon. Even if her parents were in their nineties, they'd still be crawling around the floor with their grandchildren.

She sprinkled cheese on the top layer of the lasagna. "This looks impressive. Do you think Dad will know who cooked it?"

"He won't mind. As long as there's garlic bread on the table, he'll be happy."

Sam knew for a fact that she hadn't included garlic bread on her shopping list. "Oops."

The front doorbell rang. "I'll get it." Sam wiped her hands on her apron.

"If the neighbor's children are selling chocolate, we'll have two bars."

Sam opened the door. Her smile disappeared.

Caleb stood in front of her, holding a bouquet of pale pink roses.

She held onto the door. "What are you doing here?"

"I came to see you."

Her knees were getting weaker. "I thought you were in Washington, D.C.?"

Caleb stepped closer. "I came home early. I wanted to tell you—"

Sam's mom walked into the hallway. "I brought my purse —" She looked at their visitor and a smile broke across her face. "Caleb! It's good to see you." She rushed forward and pulled him into the house. "What were you thinking, Samantha? The poor man is freezing. And he brought you roses, too."

Sam was in trouble now. Her mom was a sucker for any man who brought a woman flowers. And if that woman was her unmarried, thirty-one-year-old daughter, she wasn't letting him go.

Caleb handed Sam the roses before her mom whisked him into the kitchen. In next to no time, he was sipping coffee and telling them about the Christmas lights in Washington, D.C.

All Sam could do was sit on a stool and listen to the conversation going on around her.

"You must stay for dinner," Elena said as she refilled Caleb's cup. "We've made lasagna. It's one of our favorite recipes."

Caleb smiled. "It's one of my favorites, too."

A blush heated Sam's face. She remembered the cooking lesson Caleb had given her, the way he'd patiently shown her how to make the cheese and tomato sauces. She'd enjoyed spending time with him. And, regardless of what had happened, she missed him.

"Sam has been learning to cook a lot of our favorite recipes. Wait until you try her mini calzones stuffed with pepperoni, pesto, and ricotta. They're delicious."

"I can't wait."

Caleb's slow smile made Sam sigh. She needed to talk to him before her mom started planning their wedding.

She took off her apron and stood beside Caleb. "I forgot

to buy garlic bread. Do you want to come to the supermarket with me?"

For a moment, she thought he was going to stay with her mom. He'd see her baby photos, the pictures she'd painted in elementary school. And if her mom became really sentimental, a lock of her baby hair.

She tugged at his uninjured arm. "You really need to come with me."

Caleb's smile melted her heart. "I thought you'd never ask."

And just like that, she fell in love with him all over again.

"THIS ISN'T A SUPERMARKET." Caleb peered through the windshield at the large building in front of them. In fact, the ranch supply store was the complete opposite. "They won't sell garlic bread."

Sam smiled. "I know. Mom wants to decorate her house in tinsel and fairy lights. She said Shelley bought her decorations from Murdoch's. It's on our way to the supermarket, so I thought we could have a look."

"Are you trying to keep me away from your mom?"

"You know what she's like."

The soft blush on Sam's face made his heart race. He not only knew what her mom was like, he was hoping she might have some influence on her daughter.

Caleb undid his seatbelt. "Your mom has a heart of gold."

"Wrapped in tulle and confetti," Sam muttered. "Let's go."

As soon as they entered the store, Caleb knew they wouldn't be leaving anytime soon. If Sam wanted to buy her parents some Christmas decorations, then she couldn't go wrong here.

Sam's mouth dropped open. "It looks like Santa's cave."

Pine garlands with sparkling red berries decorated the walls. On their left were at least a dozen Christmas trees decorated with fairy lights and tinsel.

"Mom would love this." Sam touched a small tree covered in gold tinsel. "This must be what Shelley bought for her house."

"Is it the tree or the tinsel you like?"

"The tinsel. Mom wants to decorate her living room in gold tinsel and fairy lights. She'll use the same tree from last year."

Caleb walked farther into the store, searching the shelves for tinsel. It looked as though Murdoch's sold everything from cowboy boots to twine. And hats. Rows and rows of cowboy hats in every style and color imaginable.

"You should buy this one." Sam took a black hat off the stand. She stepped closer and placed it on his head. "Almost like Cinderella. It fits perfectly."

He wasn't sure a cowboy hat compared all that well to a glass slipper, but he wasn't complaining. Reaching out, he gently held Sam's hand in his. "I've missed you."

She didn't step away or tell him he was crazy. "I've missed you, too. How long are you staying in Bozeman?"

He took a deep breath. "I can stay for as long as you need me." The last thing he expected was for tears to fill her eyes. He cupped the side of her face with his hand. "Are you all right?"

Sam nodded, then shook her head.

"Was that a yes or a no?"

"It's both." She took a deep breath. "My PTSD has come back. I'm okay most of the time, but sometimes I cry."

"Like now?"

A gentle smile softened her face. "Like now. It doesn't mean I'm sad, it just means I'm crying."

"Can I do anything to help?" Caleb knew what he wanted to do. But hugging Sam might make her cry even more.

She held his hand in hers. "I'll be okay in a few minutes. Why did you want to see me, Caleb?"

This wasn't how he'd imagined telling Sam he loved her. There had to be a rule about including romantic music, candlelight, and roses. At least he'd covered the rose option—even if she hadn't realized why he was giving them to her.

"I love you, Sam. I'm sorry I didn't trust you. I was overwhelmed by what had happened and worried that the terrorists could still hurt my sister and friends. I should have apologized straightaway for what I said, but I didn't."

She squeezed his hand. "It's okay. I'm sorry, too. I knew you were exhausted, but I kept asking questions. I should have waited until the morning to talk to you."

"Do you think we can be more than friends?"

Sam kissed his cheek. "I hope so, because I love you, too. Just be careful around Mom. She has wedding bells on her mind."

"I know a cure for that," Caleb said with a smile. "We'll dazzle her with so many Christmas decorations that she won't think of anything else for the rest of the week."

"You don't know my mom. She's a great multi-tasker."

Caleb wrapped his arms around her waist. "So are we."

"I like the way you think."

Sam's smile touched something deep inside his soul. When she leaned forward and kissed him, he forgot about the Christmas decorations, the people in the store, or anything that had happened before tonight. All he knew was that he loved Sam with a force that went beyond anything he'd ever known. And he wanted to spend the rest of his life showing her just how much she meant to him.

. . .

THREE WEEKS Later

"ARE you sure you want to do this?"

Sam clenched her jaw and nodded. "I'm facing my fears and doing it anyway." She'd repeated the same words to herself all morning. Not that it was making any difference. For the last two weeks, she'd worked her way through a list of things that scared her. So far, she'd cuddled a big black hairy tarantula, patted a snake, and watched two horror movies.

Falling in love with someone who liked spine-chilling, heart-leaping, scare-fests, had been a serious mistake. After watching two of Caleb's favorite movies, she'd downloaded a copy of Pretty Woman. Thankfully, Julia Roberts and Richard Gere had banished any lingering images from the scary movies.

Today's excursion into her deepest, darkest fears involved sitting on a chairlift as it whisked her to the top of Lone Mountain in the Big Sky Resort.

Caleb had no fear of heights. He didn't see a problem with climbing onto his roof, standing on the top of a ladder, or even looking over the edge of a cliff. But for Sam, riding to the top of one of the most spectacular ski fields in Montana would be a nightmare.

To his credit, Caleb was waiting patiently beside her. They were taking one of the last chairlifts of the day to the top of the mountain. After they came down, they'd enjoy dinner with her family at the Big Sky Resort. Her sisters had offered to meet her at the top of the mountain, but if she was going to face her fears, she wanted to do it with the least number of people watching her.

"How do you feel?" Caleb asked

Sam took a deep breath. "Like I've run three marathons in a row and I still haven't reached the finishing line."

"You'll be okay. I'll be right beside you the whole time."

That's what worried Sam the most. Caleb wasn't a big man, but he was tall. One wrong move and they could plummet to the ground. "Do you promise not to make the chairlift wiggle?"

Caleb's eyes widened. "Do I look like the type of boyfriend who would do that?"

"You might point something out to me and jiggle the seat by mistake."

"I promise to keep all jiggling to a minimum."

Sam looked at him to make sure he wasn't smiling. Facing her fears was a serious business. Especially when she would be hanging in the air for eight minutes.

She checked her watch. If she didn't move soon, the ride would close for the day and she wouldn't have made it to the top of the mountain.

Grabbing Caleb's hand, she pulled him into the line of people waiting to use the lift.

"The worst part is getting on the chair," Caleb murmured. "Once we're in the air, it's easy. All you'll need to do is hold on to me."

"Is that supposed to be reassuring?" Three children in front of them slid into a chair. They made it look so easy. Sam's heart pounded as she stood on the red line waiting for their turn.

Caleb's hand tightened around hers. "Open your eyes. You'll need to see the chair."

She risked a quick glance behind her and nearly freaked out. A chair was lumbering toward them, ready to scoop them up, and dump them on the ground.

"That's it," Caleb soothed. "Bend your knees. You're sitting in a normal chair. Relax."

Sam let out a short, sharp squeal as the chair hit the back of her legs.

"Sit!" Caleb bellowed from beside her.

Between Caleb's voice and the safety bar he yanked down, she was in the chair, zooming toward an early death.

"That wasn't so bad, was it?"

Sam wasn't listening to him anymore.

Caleb chuckled. "It's not called facing your fears if your eyes are closed."

"We're a long way from the ground." Sweat trickled down her spine. It was just as well she'd worn gloves. Otherwise, her hands would have slipped off the safety bar.

"Just open your eyes a little bit. The view is incredible."

Sam took a deep breath and opened her eyes. Even wearing sunglasses, the glare from the snow-covered mountains made her squint. They were high. Higher than she thought. She tightened her hold on the safety bar and prayed they made it to the top of the mountain.

"It's amazing, isn't it?" Caleb was in his element. He loved being outside with nothing except fresh mountain air between him and the hard-packed ground.

Sam pushed her body into the back of the chair. "It's great."

Caleb rested his hand on hers. "When you see the view from the top of the mountain, it will be worth all this stress. You're very brave."

"I don't feel brave." If Sam had to describe how she was feeling, she'd say terrified. Sitting on the chairlift was like being inside a giant bubble—one that could pop at any minute.

"We're nearly halfway there. When we get to the top, let go of the bar and hold my hand. We can step off together."

After the trauma of getting on the lift, Sam wasn't looking

forward to getting off. But at least she'd be standing on the ground afterward.

"We should talk about something to take your mind off the ride."

"My brain isn't working very well at the moment," Sam whispered. "Ask me a question."

"Are you enjoying splitting your working week between Bozeman and Sapphire Bay?"

The chairlift juddered. Sam shrieked.

"It's all right," Caleb said. "It's the wind."

She practiced her relaxation breathing technique. It didn't make any difference.

"Work, Sam. Think about work."

"I don't know how long…" Another gust of wind shook their chair. "…how long I can keep managing my team and working in two locations. But it's okay for now."

"Would it make it easier if I moved to Bozeman?"

"Probably, but I'm thinking about doing something different."

Someone in a chair in front of them screamed. Sam held her breath, wondering if they'd fallen off their chair.

"It's just some kids being stupid," Caleb growled. "You'd think they'd have more respect for everyone else."

Sam would have smiled if she weren't dangling in the air. "You sound like a grumpy old man."

Caleb huffed. "Not so much of the old. I'm not forty, yet."

"It's getting closer."

"So is the top of the mountain. Are you ready to let go of the bar?"

"No." Sam's voice quivered.

"You'll be fine. See…the chairlift is slowing down. Take your hands off the bar and hold onto my hand."

She gripped Caleb's hand as if she were hanging off the

edge of a mountain. Which she was, but she was in a chairlift, and she was going to be okay. Really okay.

A few seconds later, she stood beside Caleb and breathed a sigh of relief. "We made it."

Caleb wrapped her in a hug. "You did well. I'm proud of you."

Sam leaned against him, absorbing his strength when her legs felt like rubber. "I guess we'd better have a look at the view before we go back to the resort."

For the first time since they'd left Bozeman, Caleb seemed nervous. "There's a viewing platform over here."

Riding the chairlift at this time of the day had been a great idea. Most of the people who were coming up the lift didn't stay to look at the view. They moved off to one side, then skied down the slippery slope to the bottom of the mountain.

The closer they came to the platform, the less sure Sam was about standing on it. "This would be romantic if I could enjoy the view from here." She peered over the top of her sunglasses, hoping Caleb got the hint.

"You wanted a photo of us standing on the viewing platform."

"I've changed my mind."

Caleb seemed distracted. He looked nervously toward the café.

"Are you feeling okay?"

"I need a hot chocolate."

"That sounds good to me, too." Sam was all for delaying the inevitable photo on the platform. Her only worry was that drinking hot chocolate wouldn't sit well with her nervous tummy.

As they walked toward the café, she smiled. "Look over there, Caleb. Can you see the skiers?" She pulled out her cell phone and took a photo of some people zig-zagging down another trail. Their brightly colored jackets looked like multi-colored polka dots scattered across white satin. "Do you think that's enough evidence to prove I've been here?"

Caleb studied the photo. "It could have been taken anywhere. Why don't I take your photo inside the café? Shelley and Bailey will recognize the building."

"Does this mean I don't have to stand on the platform?"

"You can stand wherever you like."

Sam did a happy dance. No platform, no plunging to her death on the jagged rocks. All she had to do was travel down the mountain on the chairlift. Yippee.

She had to remind herself that she wasn't the only person stretching their comfort zone. Caleb and her sisters had made lists of the things they were afraid to try. Sam and her sisters were keeping a scrapbook of their adventures and giving it to their parents for their wedding anniversary.

So far, they'd all checked off at least three things on their lists.

"I wonder how Bailey's figure-skating class is going."

"I'm sure she'll have lots of photos to show us." Caleb opened the café door.

Sam took off her sunglasses and stared, open-mouthed, at the people sitting in front of them. "I thought we were meeting in a couple of hours in Big Sky?"

Her mom smiled. "Caleb invited us here for dinner."

Shelley and Bailey were sitting opposite their mom and dad. Everyone seemed slightly stressed.

"It's okay," Sam reassured them. "We made it up the mountain alive. I'm just not sure if going down will be any easier."

"You could always ski to the bottom," Bailey said.

The thought of zooming down the mountain on a pair of skis horrified Sam. "I'm not skiing anywhere. I prefer to have both feet firmly on the ground. Or in the air, if that makes sense." She looked at her family and frowned. "You all look worried. What aren't you telling me?"

Caleb cleared his throat.

"I didn't have skiing on my list," she squeaked. "I don't care how many spiders I have to hold, I'm not strapping a pair of skis onto my feet."

"No one's skiing down the mountain," Caleb said softly. "I wanted to ask you something."

Before Sam realized what he was doing, Caleb knelt on one knee.

Everyone in the café stopped talking. The waiters stopped moving between the tables. Even the coffee machine blew a final hiss of steam into the air.

And Sam's heart nearly stopped beating.

"I love you, Sam. I never thought I'd find someone to share my life with, someone who loves me as much as I love them. You've always accepted me for who I am and helped me become the man I'd like to be. I can't imagine living my life without you, and I hope you feel the same way."

Sam's eyes filled with tears. "I love you, too, Caleb."

Elena pulled out a tissue and blew her nose.

Ted wrapped his arm around his wife's shoulders and kissed her cheek.

If it weren't for Bailey and Shelley's encouraging smiles, Sam would probably be a nervous wreck by now.

Caleb took a small black box out of his pocket.

The collective sigh around the café made Sam's heart clench tight.

When he opened the lid, her eyes widened. Nestled against the black satin lining was a stunning solitaire diamond ring.

"It's beautiful."

"I'm glad you like it." Tears fell down his face. "I've waited my whole life for you, Sam. I don't want to wait a minute longer. Samantha Maria Jones, will you marry me?"

She held Caleb's hands. "I would love to marry you."

"Yes?"

She nodded and smiled. "Yes."

Sam's mom burst into tears. "Oh, my goodness. I'm so happy for you both." She rushed across to them and hugged Sam and Caleb tight. "Just promise me you won't cancel your wedding at the last minute."

"Oh, Mom!" Shelley dropped her head into her hands.

Bailey patted her sister on the back. "It's okay. No one can be perfect all the time."

Between the claps and cheers from the other people in the café, Ted joined his wife. "Congratulations, Caleb. It will be good to have another man in the family. Too many females can be a little overpowering sometimes."

Elena grinned. "That's what you get when you raise strong, independent women."

Caleb held onto Sam's waist. "I'll keep that in mind when we have children."

He couldn't have said anything that would make Elena happier. She gave Caleb another hug and wiped fresh tears from her eyes.

As Sam hugged her sisters, she felt incredibly blessed. Her family meant the world to her. To have them here, at the beginning of one of the most amazing journeys of her life, was very special.

"Do you want to hug your fiancé again?" Caleb whispered from beside her.

Sam grinned. "As long as I don't have to ski down the mountain, I'll do anything for you."

"No skiing. I promise."

"In that case, I'd love to hug you." Sam wrapped her arms around him and held him close. He was her beginning, her

213

middle, and her end. She couldn't imagine spending the rest of her life with anyone else. With Caleb, she'd found the kind of love that only happened once in a lifetime. And she'd treasure it for as long as she lived.

THE END

THANK YOU

Thank you for reading *Once In A Lifetime.* I hope you enjoyed it! If you did…

1. Help other people find this book by **writing a review.**
2. Sign up for my **new releases e-mail**, so you can find out about the next book as soon as it's available.
3. Come like my **Facebook** page.
4. Visit my website: **leeannamorgan.com**

Do you want to meet Megan, Caleb's sister? Keep reading for a sneak peak of ***A Christmas Wish*** Megan and William's story. Download your copy today!

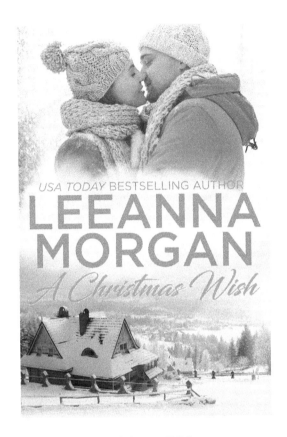

A Christmas Wish
Sapphire Bay, Book 3

Can a little girl's Christmas wish come true?

After a tragic accident, Megan is determined to give Nora, her five-year-old niece, a loving and stable home. With her fantasy cake business thriving and her niece's nightmares finally over, her life is more stable than it has ever been-- until a stranger knocks on her door and warns her that her life is in danger.

. . .

FBI Special Agent William Parker knows what it's like to lose the people you love. He's convinced himself that his job is all he needs to be happy. But while he's protecting Megan and Nora from a brutal terrorist group, his emotionless and solitary life is torn to shreds. With Christmas fast approaching, can Megan and Nora convince him that it's safe to love again…even if loving them is harder than letting them go?

Turn the page to read the first three scenes in *A Christmas Wish*, Megan and William's story.

CHAPTER 1

"*R*emember your jacket," Megan said as she picked up Nora's backpack.

Nora raced out of the kitchen. "Got it," she yelled from the living room.

Sometimes, Megan forgot her niece was only five years old. Nora was a fiercely independent little girl and wanted to be part of everything. And today, that included delivering a birthday cake to one of Megan's friends.

Nora ran back into the kitchen, dragging her jacket behind her. "I need Dolly."

Dolly was a red-headed rag doll that Megan's sister had bought Nora before she was born. It didn't matter how many times Megan stitched Dolly's seams, or carefully hand-washed her cotton body, nothing would make her last forever.

"Put on your jacket and I'll find Dolly." Megan ran upstairs and found the rag doll tucked under Nora's blankets. She took the quick find as a good sign. Sometimes Dolly ended up in the oddest places, making any exit from the house a lot longer than it should have been.

With Dolly in one hand and Nora holding the other, Megan made her way toward the garage. November in Milwaukee wasn't for the fainthearted. Bitter nor'westers blew across the yard, creating flurries of fresh snowflakes. Today was so cold that she could taste the ice on Lake Michigan. It mingled with the smoky scent of pine, oak, and spruce coming from her neighbors' chimneys. It was the Milwaukee she remembered. The city she loved.

With Christmas not far away, Megan had an enormous amount of work to get through. After two years, her fantasy cake business was finally taking off. But, with only herself to fill the orders, life could get hectic very quickly. Especially with a five-year-old running around the house.

She buckled Nora into her seat and ran to the other side of the car. "Are we ready?"

Nora waved Dolly in the air. "We ready," she yelled.

With a two-tier dragon cake sitting in the trunk and an excited little girl in the back seat, Megan reversed out of the garage. As a Bob Dylan song played on the radio and Nora cuddled Dolly, Megan smiled. Life didn't get much sweeter than this.

WILLIAM PULLED AWAY from the curb. As he drove along North Second Street, he kept his truck three vehicles behind the small red car that had reversed out of the driveway.

For the last week he'd been watching Megan Stevenson and her niece. It wasn't the most exciting assignment he'd ever had, but it was necessary. Her situation was more complicated than some of the others his team was observing, but that didn't mean it made her any safer.

Megan lived the kind of life that never drew anyone's attention. She ran her own business from home, had a small group of close friends, and spent more time at activities for her niece than in doing something for herself.

On the surface, she didn't appear to be anyone the FBI would be interested in. But sometimes, the people you least expected caused the most issues.

Megan's car turned right into East Vine Street. She'd been here before. One of her friends lived in a brick and plaster apartment halfway along the street. Sure enough, she stopped in front of her friend's home.

William slowed but kept driving. As Megan opened the driver's door, she didn't appear to notice him. Had she always been this careless about what was going on around her? He was good at his job but, after four days of being followed, she should have known he was there.

As soon as he could, he made a U-turn, parking his truck a short distance from the house. Reaching for the camera on the passenger seat, he pointed it toward her car.

He already had enough photos for the FBI, but he wasn't taking any chances. Tomorrow, he was flying back to Montana. Megan would be on her own and more vulnerable because of the little girl. Anything he documented might save her life, especially if the terrorist group found her.

Megan's brother was creating one of the most advanced military defense systems of the twenty-first century. A terrorist group had threatened to kill him. Now she was in danger because of her connection to a brother she didn't even know existed.

MEGAN CARRIED the cake box inside.

Her friend, Sarah, held tightly onto Nora's hand, opening all the doors as they made their way into the kitchen.

"Did the cake survive its journey across town?" Sarah asked.

Megan placed the box on the counter. She hoped so. It had taken two days to decorate the cake. Most of the individual elements could be fixed but, if the dragon's wings were damaged, it would be disastrous.

Holding her breath, she lifted the lid. "It's perfect. Would you like to have a look?"

Nora tugged Sarah's hand. "You have to be careful. No touching."

"I'll remember. Would you like to look at the cake with me?"

Nora's head bobbed up and down.

Megan pulled a kitchen stool out from the counter. From this distance, Nora's little fingers couldn't touch the icing. But she was close enough to still feel as though she was part of the unveiling.

The dragon birthday cake was for Sarah's husband, Josh. With bright blue and green buttercream scales, sparkling eyes, and purple candy melt wings, it sat majestically on a rocky ledge made from chocolate. Apart from seeing the cake, there was another surprise that no one would be expecting. Cradled beneath one of the dragon's wings was a golden egg. Megan thought the way Sarah wanted to tell her husband she was pregnant was adorable.

"Oh, my goodness. It's just like the picture I gave you." Sarah hugged her. "I love what you did with the egg. It looks incredible."

"Do you think Josh will get the connection between the egg and becoming a dad?"

"I hope so. If he doesn't, I'll give him some hints." Sarah continued to admire the cake, pointing out her favorite things to Nora. After she'd finished, they carefully carried it into the living room.

In the next hour, Josh's friends and family would arrive for his surprise party. About half an hour later, Josh would come home from work. Megan couldn't wait to see his face when everyone yelled, 'happy birthday'.

Sarah carefully placed a cover over the cake. "You do realize I'm paying you for this."

Megan sighed. They'd had this discussion before, and her answer had been the same. "You're not paying me. I loved making this for you and Josh. It's my way of saying thank you for everything you've done for us."

She could only imagine what her life would have been like if Sarah hadn't been here.

"We only did what anyone else would have."

They'd done so much more. Returning to Milwaukee after her parents and sister were killed in a car accident had been terrible. Even though her heart had been torn in two, she'd done her best to look after Nora.

Sarah had been her rock, her shoulder to cry on, and her safe place to fall. Nothing Megan could say or do would ever be enough to repay her kindness. But Josh's birthday cake was a good place to start.

LATER THAT EVENING, when everyone else was enjoying Josh's party, a cold chill ran down Megan's spine. She didn't know what was wrong with her. For the last couple of days, she'd had the feeling someone was watching her. It didn't matter where she was or how many people were around her, something was making her nervous.

"Are you okay?" Sarah asked. "You look as though you've seen a ghost."

She shook her head, trying to get rid of the uneasy feeling. "I'll be okay. I must have been standing in a draft."

Sarah looked behind her and frowned. "Maybe you need a hot drink. Josh's mom brought alcohol-free eggnog with her. Why don't you have a cup?"

"That sounds like a great idea. I'll find Nora and see if she'd like something to drink, too."

"She'll be okay. I saw her a couple of minutes ago with one of my sister's nieces. They were playing on the landing with their dolls."

Megan looked across the room at the staircase.

"Don't fret," Sarah said as she wrapped her arm around Megan's waist. "She'll be okay."

"I know she will. It's just that I—"

"Worry too much. Let her be a little girl. She needs to learn how to be independent."

"But she's only five years old."

Sarah nudged her across the room. "Before you know it she'll be nineteen and going away to college. She'll be all right."

Megan knew she was overprotective but, after her sister and parents died, she wasn't taking any chances with Nora.

"I know that look," Sarah said with a sigh. "Come on. We'll check on Nora before we find the eggnog. Does that sound better?"

"Much better." Megan didn't know when she would stop worrying about Nora, but she guessed 'never' would probably cover everything.

They wound their way through the room, finally making their way up the staircase. Nora wasn't there. Megan frowned at the two young girls who were playing with their dolls. "Have you seen Nora?"

"She went to look at the stars," one of the girls said.

Megan's heart raced. The temperature had plummeted. If Nora had gone outside, she could get hypothermia or—

Sarah's hand landed on Megan's arm, but her friend's

attention was focused on the little girl who had spoken. "Where did Nora go, Marianne?"

The little girl pointed to one of the bedrooms. "That way. She said that was the best room for looking at the stars."

"Thank you," Megan said as she hurried down the hallway. She opened the door and breathed a sigh of relief. Nora was curled in a ball, sound asleep on the window seat.

Sarah must have seen the look on her face. "I told you so," she whispered. "Nora is okay."

"This time she was okay," Megan whispered back. "I shouldn't have let her out of my sight."

With a smile, Sarah handed her a fluffy blanket. "Wrap this around her. When you're ready, come downstairs. I'll have your glass of eggnog waiting."

"I won't be long." Megan opened the blanket and gently placed it over Nora. With a heavy heart, she sat on the edge of the window seat and watched her niece as she slept.

Nora had her mom's cute button nose and the same big, blue, mischievous eyes that could light up a room. Sometimes, she was so much like Christine that it made Megan cry.

She glanced at the floor and picked up a sheet of paper.

Nora turned over and sent her a sleepy smile. "You found my Christmas wish."

Megan angled the picture toward the light. Two big stick people and one little one held hands in a field of flowers. The sun shone down from a clear blue sky, and a star twinkled overhead.

"I want a daddy for Christmas," Nora whispered. "You said if I was a good girl, I could ask Santa for anything."

"Santa doesn't make daddies," Megan said softly. "But he has lots of other wonderful things in his workshop."

"I want a daddy." Nora snuggled under the blanket and closed her eyes. Within minutes she was sound asleep.

Megan took a deep breath. It wasn't the first time Nora had said she wanted a father. And each time it happened, she was even more unsure about what to do.

Three years ago, Nora was happily living with her mom and grandparents in Milwaukee.

Megan was living in Dallas, working in a job she loved, and engaged to a man who meant the world to her.

In one horrific moment, everything changed. And it had never been the same since.

≈

Two days later, William sat in Caleb Andrews' living room in Sapphire Bay. The flight to Montana had taken hours, but it was important to be here. He was trying to piece together a relationship that, until a few days ago, Caleb knew nothing about.

Caleb had always thought he was an only child. Four months ago, while the FBI was investigating the families of the people in his top-secret team, they'd found Megan.

When a terrorist organization started sending death threats to the people on the team, the FBI was asked to make sure no one, including family members, was harmed.

William was here to find more proof that Caleb and Megan were brother and sister. Another team of special agents would arrive soon to provide Caleb with additional security.

He opened a folder and handed Caleb a photograph of a two-story house. "Have you seen this building before?"

Caleb studied the photo. "No. Is it important?"

"It's the house Megan lived in until she went to college."

"What did she study?"

William didn't have to look at his notes. He'd memorized her profile until he knew the details of her life as well as his own. "She went to UCLA and completed her undergraduate degree in comparative literature. Until three years ago she was a high school teacher in Dallas."

Caleb's eyes widened. "A teacher? Have you told her she might be my sister?"

"Not yet. We need more proof that you're related to each other before we approach her." At the moment, the only documents linking the two siblings was a photograph and a letter in Megan's adoption papers.

"So there's still a chance we're not brother and sister?"

There was no doubt in William's mind that they were related, but he wasn't prepared to tell Caleb until he had a DNA match. Even without the information he'd already found, Caleb and Megan looked similar. They had the same oval-shaped face, the same vibrant blue eyes and a similar shade of dark brown hair.

"There's always a possibility that she's not your sister. What we do know is that Megan is four years younger than you are and the terrorist group is watching her." He pointed to the timeline they'd been working on. "Where was your father around this time?"

Caleb leaned forward and focused on the chart. "My father was in prison. Mom had started the divorce process by then."

"How old were you?"

"About four years old."

It was possible that Caleb didn't remember his mom being pregnant. But there was a higher probability that his dad had fathered a child with someone else. "Do you have any photos of your mom around this time?"

"I'm not sure. I'll have to look through my photo albums."

"I'd appreciate you looking. If you find your birth certificate or any documents relating to your parents' divorce, they would be useful, too." William checked his watch. "We've been going over your family history for the last hour. I think it's time we had a break."

Caleb picked up a photo of Megan. "If we are related, what do you think she'll say when she finds out she has a brother?"

"She'll be as surprised as you were." William closed the folders on the table. "While I'm here, I'll check the ranger's house that Fletcher security found. I want to make sure you'll be safe if something happens."

Caleb handed him the photo. "I'll call Jeremy, one of Fletcher Security's staff, and ask him to drive you there."

"Don't worry. I'll take my truck. It's only fifteen minutes away." He needed time to think about what Caleb had told him, especially if Megan's adoption wasn't as straightforward as he'd imagined.

AVAILABLE NOW!

ENJOY MORE BOOKS BY LEEANNA MORGAN

Montana Brides:

Book 1: Forever Dreams (Gracie and Trent)

Book 2: Forever in Love (Amy and Nathan)

Book 3: Forever After (Nicky and Sam)

Book 4: Forever Wishes (Erin and Jake)

Book 5: Forever Santa (A Montana Brides Christmas Novella)

Book 6: Forever Cowboy (Emily and Alex)

Book 7: Forever Together (Kate and Dan)

Book 8: Forever and a Day (Sarah and Jordan)

Montana Brides Boxed Set: Books 1-3

Montana Brides Boxed Set: Books 4-6

The Bridesmaids Club:

Book 1: All of Me (Tess and Logan)

Book 2: Loving You (Annie and Dylan)

Book 3: Head Over Heels (Sally and Todd)

Book 4: Sweet on You (Molly and Jacob)

The Bridesmaids Club: Books 1-3

Emerald Lake Billionaires:

Book 1: Sealed with a Kiss (Rachel and John)

Book 2: Playing for Keeps (Sophie and Ryan)

Book 3: Crazy Love (Holly and Daniel)

Book 4: One And Only (Elizabeth and Blake)

Emerald Lake Billionaires: Books 1-3

The Protectors:

Book 1: Safe Haven (Hayley and Tank)

Book 2: Just Breathe (Kelly and Tanner)

Book 3: Always (Mallory and Grant)

Book 4: The Promise (Ashley and Matthew)

The Protectors Boxed Set: Books 1-3

Montana Promises:

Book 1: Coming Home (Mia and Stan)

Book 2: The Gift (Hannah and Brett)

Book 3: The Wish (Claire and Jason)

Book 4: Country Love (Becky and Sean)

Montana Promises Boxed Set: Books 1-3

Sapphire Bay:

Book 1: Falling For You (Natalie and Gabe)

Book 2: Once In A Lifetime (Sam and Caleb)

Book 3: A Christmas Wish (Megan and William)

Book 4: Before Today (Brooke and Levi)

Book 5: The Sweetest Thing (Cassie and Noah)

Book 6: Sweet Surrender (Willow and Zac)

Sapphire Bay Boxed Set: Books 1-3

Sapphire Bay Boxed Set: Books 4-6

Santa's Secret Helpers:

Book 1: Christmas On Main Street (Emma and Jack)

Book 2: Mistletoe Madness (Kylie and Ben)

Book 3: Silver Bells (Bailey and Steven)

Book 4: The Santa Express (Shelley and John)

Book 5: Endless Love (The Jones Family)

Santa's Secret Helpers Boxed Set: Books 1-3

Return To Sapphire Bay:

Book 1: The Lakeside Inn (Penny and Wyatt)

Book 2: Summer At Lakeside (Diana and Ethan)

Book 3: A Lakeside Thanksgiving (Barbara and Theo)

Book 4: Christmas At Lakeside (Katie and Peter)

The Cottages on Anchor Lane:

Book 1: The Flower Cottage (Jackie and Richard)

Book 2: The Starlight Café (Andrea and David)

Book 3: The Cozy Quilt Shop (Shona and Greg)

Book 4: A Stitch in Time (Laura and Joseph)

BONUS RECIPE - CALEB'S CHOCOLATE CAKE

Try Caleb's chocolate cake - it's delicious!

(From addapinch.com)

Ingredients:

2 cups granulated sugar

1 3/4 cups all-purpose flour

3/4 cup unsweetened cocoa powder

1 1/2 teaspoons baking powder

1 1/2 teaspoons baking soda

1 teaspoon salt

2 large eggs

1 cup buttermilk

1/2 cup oil (vegetable or canola oil)

2 teaspoons vanilla extract

1 cup boiling water

For the Chocolate Frosting:

1/2 cup melted butter

2/3 cup unsweetened cocoa powder

3 cups powdered sugar

1/3 cup milk

1 teaspoon vanilla extract

Directions:

1. Heat oven to 350°F. Grease and flour two 9-inch round baking

pans.

2. Stir together sugar, flour, cocoa, baking powder, baking soda and salt in large bowl.

3. Add eggs, milk, oil and vanilla; beat on medium speed of mixer 2 minutes.

4. Stir in boiling water (batter will be thin). Pour batter into prepared pans.

5. Bake 30 to 35 minutes and enjoy!

For a 9x13" one layer cake:

1. Grease 9x13" pan with non-stick cooking spray. Pour batter into prepared pan. Bake at 350 degrees F. for 35 to 40 minutes. Cool completely. Frost.

For cupcakes:

1. Line cupcake pan with paper liners and fill 2/3 full with batter. Bake cupcakes for 22 to 25 minutes. Cool completely completely before frosting. Makes 24-30 cupcakes

For the chocolate frosting:

1. Combine butter and cocoa powder.

2. Add powdered sugar, milk, and vanilla extract.

CPSIA information can be obtained
at www.ICGtesting.com
Printed in the USA
LVHW071024140623
R17788200003B/R177882PG749674LVX00003B/3